LAST DAYS IN AFRICVILLE

LAST DAYS
IN AFRICVILLE

DOROTHY PERKYNS

An imprint of
Beach Holme Publishing
Vancouver

This book is published by Beach Holme Publishing, Suite 1010, 409 Granville Street, Vancouver, B.C. V6C 1T2. *www.beachholme.bc.ca*. This is a Sandcastle Book.

The publisher gratefully acknowledges the financial support of the Canada Council for the Arts and of the British Columbia Arts Council. The publisher also acknowledges the financial assistance received from the Government of Canada through the Book Publishing Industry Development Program (BPIDP) for its publishing activities.

The Canada Council | Le Conseil des Arts
for the Arts | du Canada

BRITISH
COLUMBIA
ARTS COUNCIL
Supported by the Province of British Columbia

Editor: Jen Hamilton
Production and Design: Jen Hamilton
Cover Art: Ljuba Levstek
Author Photograph: Precision Photographic Services Ltd., Halifax, N.S.

Printed and bound in Canada by AGMV Marquis Imprimeur

National Library of Canada Cataloguing in Publication Data

Perkyns, Dorothy
        Last days in Africville/Dorothy Perkyns.

"A Sandcastle Book."
ISBN 0-88878-446-5

        1. Africville (Halifax, N.S.)—Juvenile fiction. I. Title.

PS8581.E723L38 2003   jC813'.54   C2003-906670-3

For Audrey, Eileen,
Nicholas, and Dwight

ACKNOWLEDGEMENTS

Although this book is a work of fiction, it attempts to record the experience of one girl who lived through the destruction of her home in the real community of Africville. Several locations in Halifax and all the characters, including the heroine, are figments of my imagination.

I wish to acknowledge the work of the Africville Genealogy Society in preserving personal accounts of life in Africville as they appear in the book *The Spirit of Africville*. I am particularly indebted to Terry Dixon and the late Dr. Ruth Johnson, who welcomed me to their homes. The staff of the Black Cultural Centre for Nova Scotia were friendly and helpful. *Remember Africville*, a production of the National Film Board directed by Shelagh Mackenzie, also assisted me in my research as did *Africville: The Life and Death of a Canadian Black Community* by Donald H. Clairmont and Dennis William Magill.

I greatly appreciate the work of the staff at Beach Holme Publishing, especially that of my editors, Jen Hamilton and Michael Carroll. As always, my husband, Richard, has been unfailing in his encouragement and support.

ONE

The sudden sting of something hitting her forehead jerked Selina Palmer's eyes away from the book secretly open on her lap to the scrap of tightly folded paper bouncing onto her desk. At that precise moment Miss Neill swung around from cleaning the blackboard to begin a dreaded multiplication-table test.

"Seven times nine, Selina!"

The teacher's nervous, high-pitched voice jolted Selina's hand, hovering to retrieve the note, to an abrupt midair halt.

"Seven times nine!"

Aware of the stifled giggles from the students nearby, Selina recovered enough to let her hand fall over the bit of paper before politely answering, "Sixty-three."

"Correct, but I don't expect to have to ask twice," Miss Neill snapped.

Although she kept her eyes attentively on the teacher while the random testing continued, Selina slid the note silently onto the hidden book and unfolded it. Her face flamed, and she felt sick to her stomach when she finally glanced down to read the lines of bold, uneven writing with its huge, sloping loops: "You may think you're great, but you won't feel great when we get you sometime later today."

Looking up questioningly at the rows of girls in front of her, Selina saw Doreen Briggs smirk across the aisle at Andrea Morris. Tears pricked her eyelids, so she turned toward the window, fixing her gaze on a bank of puffy white clouds riding a strong northwesterly wind across a spring sky the colour of robins' eggs. Normally she would have continued to enjoy her secret read, confident that Miss Neill wouldn't pounce on her again. Today she could only try to think of a way of avoiding her tormentors.

As the single black student in her grade six class at Mayfield School, Selina was accustomed to being left alone in her corner seat at the back of the room. Miss Neill ignored her as much as possible, never asking her more than the occasional token question. That meant Selina could pay attention to the lessons, catch up on reading, which she loved, or merely daydream.

Even though she enjoyed her freedom of choice, she still wished that at least one of the other students from her home settlement of Africville, the black community at the edge of Bedford Basin on the outskirts of Halifax, could join her in this class. There were a few in other regular classes, but many were unfortunately stuck in the auxiliary classes for slow learners. Her own transfer to her present rightful place had come as a complete surprise after years of frustrating boredom. Last October Mr. Fisk, the new school principal, had noticed her work when he taught the auxiliary class one day during the homeroom teacher's absence. He had moved her up at once.

Selina crumpled the note and put it in the pocket of her blouse. She began to twist one of her two tight braids with her right forefinger, a habit she had when nervous or upset. She was certain her hair was far too short for braids, but her grandmother, who looked after her while her parents were at work, insisted that braids were neater for school. Selina thought they made her face look pinched and skinny, so she always untied them the minute she reached home.

"No one ever looks beautiful with silly, short braids," she would whisper to her reflection in the mirror of Grandma's dresser as she shook out her wavy black hair into a softly curving frame for her oval face, with its smooth brown skin, high cheekbones, and huge brown eyes. She wished she could alter her height and limbs as easily as she did her hair, but nothing could prevent her from being two inches taller than anyone else in the class, nor replace her broad shoulders and long, muscular limbs.

If only she could be more like slim, girlish Miss Neill, who dressed even for school in lacy blouses and beautifully cut skirts. In spite of the teacher's curtness, Selina longed to win more of her approval. She always felt so big and clumsy beside the dainty, small-boned lady, with her short, fashionable, back-combed hairdo and brilliant blue eyes.

While the familiar teacher-student dialogue droned on, Selina kept her eyes fixed on the drifting clouds, hardly daring to admit something she had secretly dreaded. She had always sensed that some of the girls weren't comfortable having a black student among them, especially one who worked well and gained high grades. Until this moment she hadn't thought their dislike was strong enough to result in such a terrifying threat.

The harsh clang of the recess bell startled her. The rest of the students sprang up at once and began rooting for snacks from their desks and book bags before crowding to the front of the room, completely ignoring Miss Neill's order that they were not to move until she gave permission. Finally, with a resigned sigh, the teacher opened the door, and her charges surged past her.

Selina pretended to search for the small wax-paper package containing two of Grandma's molasses cookies until everyone else left. Normally she spent recess with Molly, her best friend from Africville. *I bet they chose today to send that note because they know Molly's not in school, and I'll be going home alone,* she thought as she slowly made her way outside.

Already most of the girls from her class were involved in a skipping game. Those waiting in line for a turn to jump in the long rope huddled more closely to whisper and nudge one another as she passed. Pretending to ignore them, Selina headed for the far end of the older students' play area, next to the section assigned to the younger grades. Here she walked slowly back and forth, always staying where she could easily be seen by the duty teacher, nibbling at the cookies to make them last as long as possible.

Selina almost jumped out of her skin when a voice behind her said, "It was a mean trick to send you that note. I don't blame you for staying out of their way. I always do."

Turning quickly, she almost collided with Rosalind

Devereau, to whom she had hardly ever spoken, even though they were both in the same class. Rosalind was so small and thin that Selina wondered how she could stay on her feet against the gusts of wind buffeting the playground. The girl had a tiny, pale face and straight, mousy hair clipped to one side of her forehead with a brown barrette. Rosalind's faded grey eyes looked up earnestly at Selina through thick-lensed glasses as she began to walk jerkily beside her.

Selina was aware that Rosalind limped a little, but now she could feel how unevenly the girl moved, her right leg striding much farther and more firmly than her left so that she seemed to hop like an injured fledgling. She also noticed how Rosalind held her left arm close to her body. The fingers of that hand were half-clenched, stiff, and twisted like a claw.

Rosalind was dressed in a coat and matching hat of the kind Selina had coveted when looking through the tempting pages of the Eaton's catalogue. They were made of cozy blue fabric, with fur trim at the collar and around the brim of the hat. Despite this elegance, the outfit did not look as attractive as Selina had imagined. Suddenly she realized why: it was soiled and faded, with grimy sleeve cuffs. She could see its original shade in a round blue spot at the front of the coat where a button was missing.

Grandma would never have sent Selina to school in anything so uncared for. Her own white blouse was spotless, and her plain navy skirt was neatly pressed. The zippered jacket over these, though a hand-me-down from a niece of her mother's employer, had been carefully washed that weekend.

Apart from the girl's name, which Selina thought

exceedingly glamorous, the only things she knew about Rosalind were that she always had her nose in a book, and that she had a long row of gold stars on the class-achievement chart. She rarely raised her hand to answer questions, though Miss Neill often praised her written work.

When the bell rang for the end of recess, Rosalind stopped in her tracks. "We'll wait a minute and join the end of the line. That way nobody will be able to push us."

By the time they took their places, the lower grades were already beginning to march forward. They moved smartly because Mr. Fisk was standing just inside the door. Selina was relieved. No one would dare misbehave under the gaze of this tall, muscular man with his kindly, weatherbeaten face.

Her relief was short-lived. As she reached the classroom door, Doreen Briggs, a sulky, overweight girl with lank, sandy hair, thrust her freckled, pudgy face into Selina's. "You just wait till after school," she snarled, her green eyes flashing. "You won't be able to hide from us then."

"Don't be so mean," Rosalind said in a surprisingly firm voice. "Leave Selina alone. She never did you any harm."

"I guess you think *you* can protect her," Doreen sneered. "That's a laugh."

At that moment Miss Neill called them to their seats. Selina whispered her thanks to Rosalind and dodged away to her desk at the back of the room. She sank into her seat, her heart pounding. How she hated Doreen, who never got her math right, but never seemed to get into trouble if her homework wasn't completed!

The last task of the morning was the writing of an

essay. Selina loved to write stories and cheered up at once when she saw that the subject, "What Easter Means to Me," was written on the blackboard in Miss Neill's elegant copperplate.

She wrote the date and title neatly at the top of an empty page in her scribbler. *Only six days to go!* she thought. Thrusting her worries aside, she settled down to fill a page in no time with an account of Africville's forthcoming Easter Sunrise Service.

After a long service in Seaview African Baptist Church, everyone will walk in a procession to the shore of Bedford Basin. Those to be baptized will dress in white robes, and the minister will immerse them in the ocean, as Christ was baptized in the River Jordan, though I think it would be warmer there. The service starts early before it is light. I may not go to bed the night before.

Later we will have our Easter egg hunt while my mother and grandmother prepare a huge dinner of turkey and ham and more pies than you can count. All our relations from miles around bring food and join in. When it is over, Uncle Eli will play the piano and we will sing hymns and our favourite songs. My grandmother is sewing me a new white dress as an Easter gift, and I thank the Lord with all my heart for such a wonderful time.

Selina paused before deciding not to write that the new white dress was being made from a wedding gown her grandmother had found at a flea market. Hannah Palmer was probably sitting at her ancient sewing machine this very moment, singing her heart out while she turned the handle.

Selina suddenly remembered that Uncle Eli, Grandma's youngest brother, was serving time in Rockhead Prison. It would be better not to mention that, either. Besides, the family was expecting him home for Easter. He was their best pianist and guaranteed to make any party swing, but for as long as Selina could remember his life had been punctuated by spells in jail. She was wondering why he never learned that helping himself to other people's property was against the eighth commandment, when the lunch bell clanged.

Quickly she picked up her scribbler, dashed to the front of the room, and laid it open on Miss Neill's desk, the first of the pile. Before anyone could stop her, she was through the door, along the corridor, and out into the open air, ignoring the teacher's question, "Where do you think you're going?"

TWO

It wasn't surprising that Miss Neill should be puzzled at Selina's anxiety to leave. The students from Africville came to school by bus, bringing their lunches with them. Today Selina felt she would choke if she had to sit in the classroom and eat the sandwiches her grandmother had prepared. Home wasn't *that* far away. With her long, strong legs she could run there and back easily in the allotted hour and ten minutes. She could also avoid spending time alone in the playground after eating and risk being bullied by Doreen and her friends when they returned from lunch at their homes near the school.

She ran the first part of the way, north along Gottingen Street, glad of the paved surface where she could take giant strides. When the rows of houses ended, there was a stretch of farmland to her left, which was part of Rockhead Prison grounds. During the summer, prisoners grew crops on this land, and sometimes Selina was even able to talk to Uncle Eli through the high fence. Today the field was deserted, with patches of thick mud appearing through slowly melting snow.

Beyond the prison grounds the paved road gave way to a rough, unpaved one, marking the beginning of Africville. Over the rooftops of the houses Selina could see Bedford Basin, Halifax's inner harbour. The wind gusting up from the water stung her face and made her cheeks glow. It seemed this expanse of ocean surrounded by low, tree-clad hills looked different every time she gazed at it. At the moment she saw it as a massive, brilliant blue silk quilt ruffled with millions of white lace frills.

Selina ran down the hill until she reached the higher of the two railway lines that sliced through the community at this point. She paused to look and listen, but there was no sound of an approaching train, so she hopped onto the track and turned left to stride from tie to tie in a well-practised rhythm.

She stayed on this upper track until she was level with the church tower, way to her right, below the lower track. Here, between the two rail lines, lay the main part of Africville referred to by the residents as "up the road." Small houses, all different from one another, were scattered over the rough hillside, their colourful walls and roofs bright in the sunshine. Whenever Selina jumped from the track at this point, she was swept along by the comforting feeling of coming home to a place where she was loved and understood, for she had known everyone in every house all her life.

Nimbly she skirted puddles and melting snow, aware of every twist and turn, until she reached her back door. Here she paused to remove her boots, nervous about having to explain her presence.

Selina's grandmother, who was humming quietly to herself as she stirred a pot on the stove, swung around immediately at the unexpected sound. She stared in surprise for a moment before saying, "What on earth are you doin' here at this time o' day? You not feelin' good?"

Although the greeting may have sounded severe, it disguised a genuine concern for her granddaughter. Bent at the shoulders, Hannah Palmer was a small woman who seemed shrunken by a lifetime of hard work. Her grizzled hair was snatched back severely into a tight knot from a face whose wrinkled skin was loosely stretched over cheek and chin bones, leaving deep hollows where there had once been young flesh.

Whenever Selina thought of her grandmother, she pictured her hovering over pots at the stove or kneading a huge mound of dough at the large kitchen table, always singing as she worked. Hannah's life was centred securely on her home and family. She rarely went anywhere except to church, where she never missed Sunday worship, Bible classes, and the ladies' sewing circle. Even though she could barely read or write her own name, she could quote long passages of the scriptures without faltering. Her pies and cookies were reckoned to be the best in Africville, and she was always the first to offer both, along with all other possible help, to anyone in need.

"I forgot my sneakers, and I may need them this afternoon," Selina murmured. "I hate eating in the classroom, anyway."

"Wash your hands and sit down," Hannah ordered, pouring soup from the pot into two bowls, which she set at one end of the table. "No doubt you left your bag lunch at school."

Selina nodded and made for the sink, where a bowl with just enough water for hand washing stood.

"Don't throw that water away," Grandma said, joining her. "I put it ready for myself. I can still use it."

Together they dried their hands on an old piece of towel hanging by the sink. Hannah cut thick slices of bread, and they sat down. Selina ate a mouthful of the soup and a bite of the bread, then realized she couldn't face any more food. Her stomach felt so tight and full that she laid down her spoon and began twisting her braid. All Selina could think about was the menacing expression on Doreen Briggs's face as she hissed her threats.

"You sure you're okay, honey?" Grandma asked, placing a hand on Selina's forehead.

"I'm fine."

"You certainly ain't. You feel hot. Maybe you're startin' a chill like young Molly."

"I got hot running home."

"Somethin' bad happen in school?"

Still twisting her braid as she fought back tears, Selina shook her head but said nothing.

"Get your work wrong?"

"No, I did well with my work."

Hannah went on eating quietly, remembering that gym lessons were usually on Tuesdays and Thursdays and today was Monday. She was troubled by Selina's obvious unhappiness but wise enough not to probe any further. "How would you like to go downtown after school?" she asked.

Selina looked up, eyes shining. "You mean it?"

"Sure do! I got on well with your frock this mornin', and now I need the lace for the trim and the ribbon for the sash. So why don't I meet you after school and we'll go right along? We'll walk there and take the tram home."

"That would be great! But it's your ladies' sewing circle this afternoon. You *never* miss that."

"I don't mind leavin' early for once. Lucky it ain't my turn to bake the squares for the lunch."

"If you're sure..." Selina said, knowing how much the weekly social event meant to her grandmother.

"Maybe you'd fetch me a pail of water before you go back to school. I got everythin' ready for supper first thing this mornin', so I'll leave it to cook slowly in the oven while we're gone. Your momma will be glad of a good hot meal when she gets home. That Mrs. James expects too much of her, keeps her workin' from dawn to dusk for precious little pay."

"Dad not coming back tonight?"

"No, he's on the Montreal run, so he won't be home till tomorrow."

Selina's mother, Lila, was the housekeeper for a family on Young Avenue, one of the wealthiest streets in Halifax's South End. Her father, Jake, was a sleeping-car porter with Canadian National Railways, a job he enjoyed and was proud to do.

Selina's stomach muscles relaxed, and she managed to eat most of her soup before slipping back into her outdoor clothes. Seizing the large pail from under the sink with one hand and picking up her sandwich with the other, she munched as she went around the side of the house to the well.

She hung the pail on the hook at the end of the rope and turned the handle to lower it into the well, listening for the familiar sound as it reached water and began filling itself. Slowly she wound it up again, her arms aching from the weight. Even though she hated this chore, she knew her family was lucky to have its own well, rather than being forced to pump water from a communal one. Molly's family had to do that. Their water was always brown and smelled like bad eggs, and they had to boil it before they could drink it.

Hannah watched her granddaughter from the window. "Somebody's done somethin' to upset her this mornin'!" she muttered under her breath. "Good thing I'll be at the school this afternoon. See if I can find out what's goin' on!"

Selina grasped the handle of the full bucket and held it at arm's length to avoid splashing herself. As she handed her burden to her grandmother, a goods train rumbled into view on the lower rail line, vibrating houses and fences as it clanked along. Trains were so much a part of Africville life that neither Selina nor Hannah gave it more than a passing glance.

With a hasty goodbye Selina strode up the hill to retrace her steps back to school, relieved she would be safe this afternoon. It wasn't until she reached the prison field that she realized she should have paid a visit to the outhouse at home. Now she'd have to wait until she reached the school. At least the washrooms there were indoors, with hot and cold water for washing your hands!

THREE

Arriving at school just as the afternoon bell was ringing, Selina was surprised to find Rosalind waiting for her on the sidewalk near the entrance to the playground. They strolled unhurriedly toward the door together, so they could again join the end of the line. This time they managed to reach the classroom without anyone speaking to them. As Selina took her seat, she began to hope the morning's threats had been merely a cruel joke. Doreen and her friends had never even glanced in her direction.

She had little time to dwell on this, because Miss Neill began passing out paper for a surprise math test. There was a chorus of outraged groans and several voices pleading "Oh, no, miss, please! We never do math after lunch!" The teacher held up her hand for silence, threatened to deduct five marks from the score of anyone uttering another word, and proceeded to write twenty math questions on the board.

The room became unusually quiet as students settled down apprehensively to tackle the questions. Selina whizzed through the first ten, which were easy addition and subtraction. Her progress was somewhat slower with the next six, multiplication and division, but she didn't pause until she reached question seventeen, which was a problem involving two calculations. She thoughtfully gazed across the room while deciding how she would write out her answers.

The students were concentrating hard, carefully copying down sums, sighing as they worked them out. Selina noticed one or two of them secretly counting on their fingers beneath their desks. Miss Neill, who was correcting the morning's essays, looked up from time to time.

Selina's attention was caught by a movement across the aisle in front of her. Doreen was holding out her ruler to Andrea Morris, taking care to keep it low, out of Miss Neill's sight. Wobbling on the end of it was a scrap of paper. Andrea grabbed the note, read it rapidly, and turned it over to scribble something on the back. She then tried to balance it on her own ruler, but it slipped off as she was passing it back. Doreen sighed and raised her eyes irritably to the ceiling. Andrea tried again, keeping her ruler level this time as she held out the note to her friend. Doreen was by now so impatient that she lunged forward to grab at it, knocking the ruler to the floor with a loud clatter.

Miss Neill leaped from her desk and strode angrily toward the two red-faced girls. "What do you think you're doing in the middle of a test?" she demanded, bending to retrieve both ruler and note.

Doreen and Andrea hung their heads but didn't

reply. Miss Neill glanced at the note as Doreen muttered, "We were only checking answers."

"Indeed! Let me see what you've done."

Leaning over Doreen's shoulder, the teacher shuddered inwardly at the girl's poor, untidy effort. If she deducted the threatened five marks, Doreen would probably score zero, and that might lead to trouble for herself. Doreen's father held a respected position at city hall and knew everyone on the school board. She was aware he had already told Mr. Fisk he would prefer his daughter to be taught by someone older and more experienced. Anxious not to give further cause for complaint, Miss Neill decided it would be wise to smooth over the incident. She thought for a moment before saying, "I'm sure you meant no harm, but checking answers with each other in a test is as bad as talking. Please remember that, both of you."

Doreen and Andrea did their best to look contrite and murmured, "Thank you, Miss Neill." As soon as the teacher turned to walk back to the front of the room, however, they grinned and winked at each other before bending purposefully over their work. Selina, too, went back to hers, though she and the rest of the class knew Miss Neill had shown unfair favouritism toward the two hateful girls.

She longed for the afternoon to be over, even finding it difficult to concentrate on her book during the half hour of silent reading that followed the test while Miss Neill wrote homework assignments on the board. Many of the students were still copying these when the final bell rang, with the result that the usual mad rush for the door was prevented.

Selina wrote as fast as she could, but by the time she

finished, Doreen and Andrea had already dashed off. Rosalind had also left and was nowhere to be seen when Selina went to pick up her coat in the cloakroom. Pushing through the heavy outer door, she stood on the top step and gazed across the playground, where a couple of younger boys were kicking a small ball to each other. There was no sign of anyone from her class, so she walked toward the gate, looking anxiously for her grandmother.

She paused on the sidewalk for a moment, wondering what to do, then took a few steps in the direction of home, expecting to meet Grandma. Suddenly she was surrounded by a mob of shrieking, laughing girls, who sprang from behind a knot of thick bushes growing on a patch of waste ground beside the school fence. They began to push her from one to the other, egged on by Doreen, who yelled, "Push her harder! Let her know what we really think of her, coming from that Africville slum and thinking she's as good as us!"

Miss Neill, who happened to open the school door at that moment, heard the commotion and recognized Doreen's voice. Having narrowly avoided trouble with the tiresome girl once that afternoon, she hastily stepped inside again, deciding it would be more convenient to leave by a different door on the opposite side of the building. After all, if there was a fight, it wasn't on school property and was therefore not her responsibility. Guiltily she hurried away, refusing to acknowledge that she might have been able to prevent someone from getting hurt.

Selina was whirled around until she dropped her book bag, which some of the girls began to kick in the dirt. Hastily she stooped to retrieve it, brushing off mud as she stood again to find herself face-to-face with

Doreen, who was swinging a doubled skipping rope, poised to strike her.

As Selina cowered, hiding the back of her head with her hands, bracing for the lash, she heard several frightened voices. "Don't do it, Doreen. You'll get us all into trouble. It's dangerous."

Selina sank to her knees and held her breath, but the cruel blow she feared never landed. Instead a familiar voice, angrier than she ever remembered hearing it, cried out, "Oh, no, you don't! I'll take the rope. Think yourself lucky I don't use it on you."

She glanced up just in time to see her grandmother grab the whirling rope and wrench it from Doreen, who turned and fled with the rest of the girls. Selina staggered to her feet.

The old lady clasped her trembling granddaughter in her arms. "You okay, honey?"

"I'm fine," Selina whispered, brushing at tears with the back of her hand.

"Then we'll be on our way."

Grandma wound up the rope neatly and pushed it into her tote bag. Tall as she was, Selina didn't pull away when Hannah took her hand as they set off. It was a comfort to feel her grandmother close.

"If there's any trouble tomorrow at school, just ask Mr. Fisk to send for me," the old lady declared.

Selina nodded, and for a while they walked in silence, through streets lined with the small, respectable homes of Halifax's North End. Finally they came to Gottingen Street, where crowds bustled along the sidewalk and storefronts were lit up and decorated with Easter bunnies, huge blue eggs, and bright yellow artificial daffodils.

To Selina's surprise Grandma ignored the familiar shops, even Harding's, where Selina's mother bought her the few clothes that weren't hand-me-downs or made over from other people's castoffs. Instead they made for Barrington Street, the heart of downtown, where the stores and businesses were more elegant than those on Gottingen. Selina could hardly believe it when they turned into Benton's, a fabric shop lined from floor to ceiling with rows of cloth bolts, all colours and textures. She gazed around in a trance. If only she could choose exactly what she wanted from such an array, instead of mere trimmings for a dress made from something a stranger had discarded.

While the salesclerk, a severe-looking, bony woman in her fifties, waited on a white customer in an expensive tailored suit and fur coat, Hannah stood silently to one side, not moving a muscle, almost as if she wished to shrink into the background. Selina sidled toward an eye-catching display of lengths of attractive floral fabric draped over a fake forsythia tree. She was secretly deciding which one she liked best when her grandmother whispered firmly, "Don't touch a thing! Stay right here beside me."

At that moment the store bell jingled and another white lady entered. She smiled warmly at Selina, who smiled shyly back, taking in the simple brown cloth coat and felt hat the woman wore. For an instant she was ashamed of Grandma's woollen cap and threadbare black coat, which hung shapelessly to Hannah's ankles. It was the only coat Selina could ever remember her grandmother owning.

With many humbly repeated thanks the clerk handed a large parcel to the smartly dressed customer. To

Selina's indignation she then turned her attention to the lady who had just entered, ignoring Grandma, who continued to stand motionless, staring into space. Selina fumed. Would her grandmother *ever* be served if the clerk always waited on any white customer who happened to drop in?

An astonishing thing happened, however. The second woman spoke up in a clear voice, indicating Grandma with her outstretched hand. "This lady was here before me. It's her turn next."

The clerk looked uneasily from the white woman to the black, but Grandma didn't budge. To Selina's dismay she stood as if rooted to the spot, murmuring that it didn't matter. The other customer was quite firm, though, and insisted with another smile that Grandma was first in line.

"Come on," Selina urged, grasping Grandma's elbow and guiding her to the counter, "tell her what we want."

Tight-lipped and scowling, the salesclerk produced some broad white ribbon of heavy satin. With an angry slash of her huge scissors, she cut off the two yards Grandma requested. Next, the clerk unrolled three samples of white lace for their inspection.

"Which do you like best?" Grandma whispered.

After examining them all, Selina chose one with a dainty pattern of seashells. As the clerk measured out three and a half yards, Selina surveyed the growing heap of fresh, new trimmings and began to feel quite proud that they could afford all these luxuries for her dress.

"How much?" Grandma asked, taking a large change purse from the deep pocket of her coat.

"The ribbon's twenty-five cents a yard," the clerk

snapped. "Lace is thirty. That'll be one dollar and seventy cents."

Selina did a rapid calculation in her head before saying firmly, "One fifty-five. You're charging us for four yards of lace. We're only taking three and a half."

Grandma's stony expression softened into a wide grin as she handed a five-dollar bill to Selina. "Good thing you're here, honey! You'd better pay, then you can check the change for me."

With a face like a thundercloud the clerk bundled the notions into a brown paper bag, counted out three dollars and forty-five cents into Selina's outstretched hand, and slammed the till shut.

As they turned to leave, the other customer smiled again and whispered, "You must be good at math in school."

"You sure gave that poker-faced hussy something to think about!" Grandma declared proudly the minute they stepped outside.

"So did that other customer, making sure we were waited on. She was real nice!"

"Sure was! That sort o' thing doesn't often happen."

"There's a number three coming!" Selina said, catching sight of an approaching tram.

They hurried to a nearby stop in time to climb aboard. The vehicle swung and rattled until they eventually passed through the area near the school. Here the sheer terror Selina had recently experienced seized her again. She felt sick and hot and started to twist her braid for comfort. Grandma watched her sadly but said nothing.

By the time the tram reached the terminus, they were the only passengers left. Selina noticed that her grandmother was unusually slow as they trudged against a driving wind toward Africville.

Hannah, who puffed and wheezed as she walked, halted abruptly to catch her breath before gasping, "I sure wish that tram could take us all the way home, but they never seen fit to pave our streets. Same as with the water and sewer. We never been considered good enough to need *them* neither. We're good enough to pay taxes, but not good enough to have all the services white folks takes for granted. There's no way we'll *ever* get them now."

Although Selina had often overheard adults complaining about these things, the resignation in Grandma's voice troubled her. It wasn't like Hannah to sound so crushed and defeated but bitterly angry at the same time.

Blessed with boundless energy, Selina never found the walk from the tram difficult. Rather, it was a special part of going home to the safety and separateness of Africville. Now that she was forced to slow her pace to that of the bent figure beside her, she began to understand what it would mean for someone of her grandmother's age to ride home in comfort.

Selina wondered fleetingly if Grandma was well, but Hannah was never sick, so she immediately pushed the thought aside. *She's probably just tired after such a long and busy day,* Selina decided, putting her arm around her grandmother and resolving to be as helpful as possible when they reached home.

FOUR

Selina woke the following morning to the murmur of a serious conversation between her mother and grand-mother. Sensing she was the subject of discussion, she slipped out of bed and crept to the top of the stairs so she could hear what was being said.

"I think I should go up to the school, Lila, and tell Mr. Fisk what I saw," Hannah insisted.

"No, Ma," came the gentler voice of Selina's mother. "It's up to Jake and me to decide what's best in a case like this. He'll be home later this morning. You can find out how he feels, but tell him I don't want anything done to spoil Selina's chances of a real good education at the school. Now I have to go, or I'll miss my tram and be late for work, and that'll put Mrs. James in a nasty temper."

Selina scooted back along the landing in time to wave to her mother from her bedroom window. Wistfully she watched the small, slight figure turn and climb the hill. Momma was fully three inches shorter than Selina and always seemed frail. If only she didn't have to work so hard all the time! Selina loved her grandmother, but there were times, like today, when she wished her mother could be the one with her to sort things out at school.

"You better get a move on," Grandma called from the bottom of the stairs, jerking Selina into action.

After a quick breakfast, she hurried away, hoping Molly would be back today, but there was no sign of her friend at the bus stop. Rosalind, though, was eagerly waiting for her in the cloakroom when she reached school, and the two of them went into class together. Doreen was not at her desk.

Halfway through math class, the secretary appeared with a message for Selina to go to Mr. Fisk's office. Her heart sank as she made her way along the corridor and knocked timidly on the principal's door. Upon entering, she was confronted by a mean-looking man in a tight brown suit. From his slicked-back sandy hair and sly green eyes, Selina spotted his likeness to Doreen, realizing with a shock that he must be her tormentor's father.

"So this is the girl!" the man shouted. "You'd better get things sorted out, Fisk, or I'll report the whole matter to the school board."

Mr. Fisk didn't reply. Instead he smiled at Selina before saying, "Mr. Briggs tells me you have a skipping rope belonging to Doreen. Is that true?"

"Well, no...I mean, yes—"

"She's as good as admitting she took it!" Mr. Briggs declared.

Again the principal ignored the other man and quietly

asked, "Why don't you explain what happened, Selina?"

When Doreen's father tried to interrupt again, Mr. Fisk held up his hand for silence while he listened attentively to Selina's hesitant but truthful account of the previous day's events. Mr. Briggs, on the other hand, snorted impatiently and shook his head in disbelief the whole time she spoke.

"Your grandmother has the rope then?" Mr. Fisk asked as soon as she finished.

"I never heard such a pack of lies in my entire life!" Briggs bellowed. "You actually believe what this girl says?"

"I've always found Selina to be absolutely truthful."

"Are you saying my Doreen is *not* truthful?"

"I suggest we ask Selina's grandmother to come and tell us what she saw," Mr. Fisk said.

"She'll back the kid up! We'll never get to the truth. You can't really believe my Doreen would send a note like that. She wouldn't want to associate with—"

"Go at once and ask your grandmother if she wouldn't mind coming over to the school," the principal interjected.

Selina sped away from the office and along the corridor, grabbing her coat from the cloakroom and slipping it on as she ran. Opening the outer door, she gasped and bowed her head and shoulders against the icy wind blowing up from the sea. She had barely reached the edge of the playground when the top of her head hit something soft but firm, forcing her to stop with a jerk. Raising her eyes, she found herself face-to-face with her father.

"Dad! What are *you* doing here?"

"And where are *you* going at this time of the morning?" Jake Palmer, still wearing his porter's uniform, put an arm around his daughter's shoulders to guide her back into school.

"I was sent to bring Grandma," Selina explained.

"I just got home from Montreal on the overnight run. When she told me what happened yesterday, I came right here. Not a minute too soon, seems to me."

Jake was tall and muscular with broad shoulders. He looked strong enough to fight anyone, though in reality he was one of the gentlest men alive. It was easy to see where Selina got her height and long limbs, though her face and hair were exactly like her mother's. Today his normally cheerful round face was clouded with an expression that was a mixture of anger and anxiety.

As they walked down the corridor, Selina explained what had happened with Doreen's father. Jake listened but offered no comment. When his daughter timidly knocked on Mr. Fisk's door and turned the handle, however, he pulled himself up to his full height and strode firmly into the room after her.

Mr. Briggs looked stunned at the sight of this proud man. He backed away and plopped into a chair, nervously tapping its arms with his short, pudgy fingers. Mr. Fisk, however, came forward with a smile to shake hands as Jake explained his presence before pulling the rope from his jacket pocket.

"I'm willing to return this to its owner," he said. "None of my family wants anything that isn't rightfully ours, but this rope must never be used to hurt Selina again, nor anyone else, for that matter."

Mr. Fisk nodded, but Mr. Briggs shouted indignantly, "You're willing to accept his excuse for his daughter's thieving? This is outrageous! Doreen would never dream of doing anyone harm."

Selina's father stepped across to Mr. Briggs and leaned over his chair, towering so far above him that the fat man seemed to shrink. He looked apprehensively up at Jake, who now produced a crumpled scrap of paper.

"Then how do you explain this?" he demanded, waving the paper in his shaking fist. "My mother found it this morning when she was doing the laundry. It was in the pocket of the blouse Selina wore to school yesterday."

Mr. Fisk examined the note before passing it to Mr. Briggs, who glanced at it and pushed aside. "She could have written it herself, or her grandmother could have!"

"I n-never..." Selina stammered.

"Ask Miss Neill to come to my office," Mr. Fisk said to Selina. "Tell her to bring one of Doreen's scribblers and one of yours."

Selina hurried to her classroom, where the students stared as Miss Neill selected two scribblers from the pile on her desk, ordered the class to continue working, and disappeared with Selina. When they reached the office, Mr. Fisk compared the note first with Doreen's scribbler, then with Selina's. Without comment he passed the scribblers and note to Mr. Briggs, who scanned them eagerly for a full a minute before leaping up to fling them onto the principal's desk. His face was the colour of a ripe tomato as he tried not to believe the evidence before him.

"You've made up your mind!" he thundered. "You really think my daughter wrote that note!"

"I'm afraid I do," the principal replied. "Miss Neill, what do you say?"

Miss Neill took a deep breath. "I'm sorry, Mr. Briggs, but it seems that way."

"It's all your fault!" Mr. Briggs shouted, unable to contain himself. "She never learns anything in your class. Her marks are always low."

"Doreen doesn't always try—" Miss Neill began.

"I want none of your excuses, nor yours, Fisk. Doreen will never set foot in this school again. I'll send her to a private school, where she'll get individual attention and be able to mix with people of her own sort." With that he turned on his heel and stormed out of the office.

Selina said a quick goodbye to her father and hurried away, anxious to catch up with her work. She sat at her desk, ignoring the inquisitive glances of the other students. A few moments later Miss Neill entered the room, accompanied by Mr. Fisk, who handed Selina an envelope and asked her to take it to the grade one teacher. Somewhat surprised, she made her way to the opposite end of the building. By the time she returned, the recess bell was ringing.

She never found out what the principal said during her absence, but she always remembered that particular recess as the start of a much happier time in her school life. The minute she set foot in the playground the girls invited her to join in their skipping game, and she was soon jumping in and out of the rope with the best of them.

It wasn't until there was a break in the game that she noticed Rosalind standing sadly alone some distance away. Her heart went out to the small, lame girl, and she ran to take her by the arm. "Don't stay on your own. Come over and watch."

As the two approached, some of the girls glanced at one another, wondering what to do. Surprisingly it was Andrea Morris who spoke up first. "Rosalind could

turn the rope. Then only *one* of us would have to."
Rosalind's tiny, serious face lit up with a huge smile as
she took hold of the rope with her good hand.

"Would you like to have lunch at my house tomorrow?" she asked Selina when they joined the line with
everyone else at the end of recess.

"If your mother doesn't mind."

"She won't know. She'll be at work."

Selina could hardly wait for the end of the day, so
that she could tell her parents and grandmother how
things had turned around for her.

The following noon she walked with Rosalind to a
quiet, tree-lined street not far from school. The houses
here were small but neat, with tiny, unfenced front
yards, where forsythia and a few crocuses were beginning to bloom. When they reached number twenty-three,
Rosalind produced a door key from a piece of string
hanging around her neck. She unlocked the door, and
they sat at the bottom of the stairs in the tiny hallway
to remove their boots. Rosalind then led the way
through the small living room toward the even smaller
kitchen.

Selina, however, stopped in the living room, astonished at the amount of furniture. There was a long
turquoise chesterfield with two matching easy chairs,
and four end tables all in shiny dark wood. China fig-
urines shared a glass-fronted cabinet with brightly
coloured cups and saucers, while an enormous pink
vase stood on the central, glass-topped coffee table.
Selina, who had admired many of these objects in the
Eaton's catalogue, had never really considered that anyone would actually own them.

"I hope you like baked beans."

At the sound of Rosalind's voice calling to her Selina hurried to the kitchen to find her friend emptying the contents of a tiny can of baked beans into a saucepan.

"I hope this is going to be enough for both of us," Rosalind said as she carried the pan to the stove.

Being used to Grandma's huge crock of home-baked beans with plenty for everyone to have as many servings as they liked, Selina was dismayed at the small amount of food.

"You can have most of it," Rosalind said, as if reading her thoughts. "I don't eat much. You can have more toast if you like." She placed two slices of store-bought bread in the toaster.

"Where's your mother?"

"At work. She manages the toy department at Eaton's."

"You have beautiful furniture," Selina remarked, seating herself on a bright new chrome-and-plastic chair beside the matching table.

"My mother likes fashionable things. She buys everything at Eaton's."

Rosalind served the beans and toast on pretty flowered plates, which Selina again recognized from her catalogue browsings.

"Where does your father work?" she asked.

"He's still in Toronto. He's a businessman."

Selina had no idea what the term *businessman* meant, but she nodded. "My father's a sleeping-car porter and my mother's a housekeeper. Will your father be home for Easter?"

For several moments Rosalind didn't reply. She turned deep red and hung her head, longing to share her secrets with her new friend. Powerful memories of bitter fights between her parents, fights for which she felt responsible, flooded her mind. At last she said, almost in a whisper, "My mother left Toronto because she and my father couldn't agree on what should be done with me."

Selina was puzzled. "What do you mean?"

"Ever since I can remember my father's wanted me to have therapy for my arm and leg. It would help me walk straight and use my hand properly, but my mother doesn't trust doctors. She blames the one who attended her when I was born for my problems. She always said I would grow out of them. Dad says nobody is to blame and I should get all the medical help I can. They had a big argument about me the Christmas before last, because he made an appointment for me without telling her. Instead of letting me see the specialist, Mother packed our cases and brought me here."

Selina didn't know how to reply, so she continued eating.

"I've never had many friends because I couldn't join in everything," Rosalind said. "Mother tries to make it up to me by buying me lots of toys and books and pretty clothes, but I'd rather she were home more and didn't..."

Selina began to feel desperately sorry for Rosalind. "Well, you've got me now, and the other kids are including you more. And when Molly comes back, you'll have her, too."

They lapsed into an uneasy silence, during which Selina admitted to herself that she was lucky always to have her grandmother at home. At last she spoke again, anxious to break the awkwardness of the moment. "I can't wait for the weekend. I love Easter, especially the big Sunrise Service."

"What's that?"

"It's the special Easter Service. We go to church first,

almost before it gets light, then we all go down to Bedford Basin for baptism. The minister immerses the people who are being baptized in the ocean as the sun comes up."

Rosalind looked horrified. "Right in?"

"Yes, so their sins are washed away, just like Christ was baptized in the River Jordan in the Bible. I guess you go to a different church."

"Not often."

"Easter is one of our biggest days. People come from miles around. All my aunts and uncles and my cousins are there. We have a great time with a party afterward. What are you doing for Easter?"

"Not too much. Mother's usually tired after work. Saturday will be one of the busiest days of the year at the store."

"Why don't you come down to Africville then? You'll have to get up real early, but you'll have no problem finding the way. Just follow the crowd."

Rosalind didn't reply immediately. Carefully she considered whether she would be able to get away without having to ask permission, which she felt would almost certainly be refused. When her mother returned from work on Saturday, she would probably make some scrambled eggs for supper. She would then take a long bath while Rosalind washed the dishes. Later she would come downstairs in a smart dress, saying she had arranged to meet some friends from work for a movie, one that wasn't suitable for Rosalind. Promising not to be late, she would leave her daughter to read or watch television on her own.

Months of this routine had taught Rosalind not to stay up, for her mother never returned until after midnight.

On Sunday she would stay in bed until lunchtime, so she would never notice if Rosalind went out early. The service would be over in time for her to be back before her mother even woke. She turned to Selina and smiled one of the rare smiles that transformed her pale face. For a few seconds she looked almost pretty.

"Thank you, I'd love to come to the Sunrise Service," she said politely.

FIVE

Selina always found the Saturday before Easter Sunday difficult, partly because she was excited about the forthcoming celebrations, partly because the whole house was in such a frenzy of preparation that no one had time to pay her much attention.

She began the morning by watching her grandmother prepare a mound of stuffing for the biggest turkey she had ever seen.

"I'll put this in the oven the minute I get up tomorrow mornin'," Hannah said. "Then it'll be good and ready after service."

"Do you know how many folks are coming?" Selina asked, helping herself to a crouton.

Grandma gently swatted her hand. "Leave that alone! You know full well we never can say how many, but they're all welcome to a good hot dinner, whether they're family or strangers."

"You can help me with these carrots," Selina's mother said.

Selina sighed and started to slice the pile of peeled carrots her mother placed on the cutting board. She hated this job. It always seemed to go on for hours. She bit into a small carrot, deciding she would go and look for Molly as soon as she could get away. To her relief her friend appeared when she was only halfway through her task.

"You can leave the rest," Lila said. "Get some fresh air. If you want to eat today, come back here and fix yourselves sandwiches with whatever you can find. You can make it up at the feast tomorrow."

"My house is stacked with food, too," Molly said. "I've been helping my mom make pies ever since I got up this morning."

"You better?" Selina asked.

"I feel fine now."

Molly was shorter and slimmer than Selina, with tight, short black curls and a happy temperament. She always seemed to be smiling, and few things worried her except math, especially at exam time.

They walked down the hill to the lower railway line, where they turned right and strode along the ties until the distant rumble of an approaching freight train sent them scrambling to the road below. The deafening clackety-clack of the long string of passing cars made conversation impossible. The girls knew without discussing it that they would make for their favourite spot beside Tibby's Pond, which was really an inlet from the sea shaped like a horseshoe. At high tide only the strongest swimmers tested their skills on hot summer days. At low tide even the most timid could enjoy a dip or play with a raft.

The afternoon was mild and dry with little wind. The

air felt good as they left the track and hurried to the far side of the pond where there were no houses. Here they flung themselves onto the grass above the shingle beach.

"School okay this week?" Molly asked.

"Began bad, ended well." Selina explained what had happened.

"You must have been scared to death."

"Yes, but Mr. Fisk sorted things out. Now that Doreen's gone the other girls are my friends."

Molly fixed her eyes on the distant shore before replying wistfully, "If you play with them at recess, you won't be able to play with me. We've always been best friends."

"We still are! No one can spoil that. Africville friends are closer than any others," Selina assured her. "I don't see why you can't play with the other kids, too."

They sat for a while in companionable silence until Molly suddenly stood and said that her mother had given her strict orders not to get chilled.

"We could go and see Aunt Margaret," Selina suggested. "She usually likes a visit."

The two girls turned inland and crossed the lower rail line again. Then they continued up the hill toward the upper track, since the house they were going to was just below this. Its owner was Margaret Trimm, an elderly, unmarried lady who lived alone. Although she had no close relatives in Africville, everyone knew and loved her and called her Aunt Margaret.

Selina and Molly knocked on the door and walked right into the kitchen, feeling certain of a welcome and a lunch. Instantly they realized this was not a good time to drop in. Every available surface was filled with dishes, while the sprightly old lady stood at the loaded kitchen table beating cake batter in an enormous bowl.

"I'm sorry I can't stop," she apologized. "I have to bake these squares, and then I've a ham to roast. I usually wind up with a house full of visitors on Easter Sunday, mostly old friends from out of town, so I've got to make sure I have enough food."

The two girls retreated with a hasty goodbye, deciding they'd better go back to Selina's. They spent the afternoon keeping out of the way in her bedroom, only hopping downstairs for snacks or a visit to the outhouse. The rest of the time they read or played board games until Molly left at nine o'clock.

Although it was bedtime, Selina was sure she'd never be able to sleep. For one thing, there was still the noise of preparations downstairs. Furniture was being moved as extra panels were slotted into the dining table to make it as big as possible. Selina knew it had been laid with a sparkling white cloth when she heard the sound of knives and forks rattling.

She must have fallen asleep before the adults came up to bed, for the next noises she heard were the creak of the stairs as someone went down them and voices in the kitchen below. It was Easter Sunday at last. She wasn't going to wait a moment longer, even though it was still dark.

Her mother was heating kettles on the stove as she entered the kitchen, while the sound of her father singing quietly came from behind a curtain across the entrance to a small scullery, where he was washing and shaving.

Lila half filled a pitcher with hot water and handed it to Selina. "Take this upstairs! Mind you scrub every scrap of yourself."

Selina carried the pitcher up to her room and poured the water into the large china bowl on her washstand. Today of all days she knew better than to skimp on washing, so she paid special attention to her ears and scrubbed her nails with a small brush. She had just dried herself and put on clean underclothes when her mother appeared.

"I thought you might need a little help," Lila said, taking the new dress from the closet.

How wonderfully rich it felt to Selina as she slid it over her head! Before her mother could even do up the back, she dashed into Grandma's room to look at herself in the mirror. For once in her life she felt truly elegant as she admired the wide satin sash and lace trimming at the neck, sleeves, and hem.

"Ma's sure done a great job," her mother said. "Turn around while I zip you up and tie a big bow with this lovely ribbon. You can go downstairs and show Dad how good you look, but then you'd better wear one of my aprons while you eat breakfast."

"I don't want any breakfast."

"You have to eat something. It's going to be a long morning."

Downstairs Grandma and her father were munching toast and marmalade at the kitchen table.

"You look beautiful, honey," Jake said as Selina stood in the open doorway. "Thanks, Ma, for such a lovely job."

Selina came forward to hug her grandmother, who hung back. "Not now, child! We don't want you gettin' marmalade all over yourself." But everyone could tell she was pleased by the smile that belied her sternness.

Selina toyed with a bowl of cornflakes, glancing at the clock every few seconds to ask, "When can we go? If we're not careful, the church will be full before we get there."

Her father went to the window and parted the drapes. "I can just see Aunt Margaret coming along. She's always the first to arrive."

"You'd better wear a sweater and a jacket," her grandmother said, "at least until you get to the church. It's chilly outdoors. I felt the wind blow right through me when I went to the outhouse just now."

"You can take them off once it begins to warm up in there," Lila assured her.

"I just remembered..." Selina said, looking panic-stricken.

"What's the matter?" Grandma asked.

"I invited a friend from school to come to church with us. I promised to meet her at the church door. How can I do that and not lose my place?"

"Who is she?" Lila inquired.

"Her name's Rosalind Devereau."

"What does she look like?" her father asked.

"She's a white girl, and she'll wear a blue coat. She's small and thin, and limps a little."

"Poor kid!" Jake said. "You three should save two extra seats. I'm on duty at the church door to greet folks as they come in, so I'll keep an eye out for Rosalind and bring her to you if she shows up."

They left the house a few moments later to find small clusters of people, dressed in their Sunday best, making their way in the grey early light toward the little church with its cream walls and red roof. The family was climbing the steps to the door when the first note of the single bell rang out.

Selina shivered as they entered, for the building was freezing and the wood of the pew struck cold through her jacket when she sat down three rows from the front. Although they were among the first to take their seats, the church filled quickly. She glanced anxiously over her shoulder from time to time, but the organist was already playing quietly before her father pushed his way through the crowd of latecomers trying to find seats. A very scared-looking, breathless Rosalind followed him, squeezing herself in beside Selina.

"It was farther than I realized," Rosalind whispered. "I thought I'd never get here."

"I'm glad you made it," Selina said, beaming.

Instantly the minister announced the first hymn and the congregation rose. Never in her entire life had Rosalind heard such hearty singing as the message of Easter pealed forth in the well-known hymn "Christ the Lord Is Risen Today." From that first moment she was caught up in the joy of the occasion and found herself happily joining in. During the prayers and the scripture readings, people sometimes called out "Halleluiah!" or "Praise the Lord!" when they were especially moved by certain passages. Although Rosalind had never encountered this kind of thing in church before, she didn't find it strange, for there was such sincerity in the way these exclamations were uttered.

After the lengthy service, the congregation filed from the church behind the baptism candidates in their white robes. They sang as they walked to Bedford Basin, which glinted in the first low rays of sunshine. Everyone crowded to the edge of the water while one by one the candidates approached the minister. Supporting them in his arms, he gently but quickly immersed them in the icy harbour, praying for each in turn. As soon as this was over, the congregation again sang joyously before the final blessing.

"Well, what did you think of the service?" Jake asked Rosalind as they finally dispersed.

"It was wonderful. I've never been to anything like it."

"Happy to have you with us!"

"Thanks, but I have to go home now."

"You can't walk all that way without somethin' to eat, child!" Grandma was horrified. "No one leaves Africville on Easter Sunday without a good hot dinner inside them."

It took a while to reach Selina's house because there was such a crowd. Everyone kept stopping to wish friends and neighbours "Happy Easter!" When they eventually opened the door, the most delicious smell of roasting turkey met them.

"Now you two girls take one each o' them baskets off the dresser and see if you can find some chocolate eggs while we cook the vegetables and make some gravy," Grandma said.

Rosalind and Selina seized two little fruit baskets that Grandma had covered with scraps of bright fabric. Shyly Rosalind followed her friend through the rooms of the house, searching behind curtains and under ornaments for tiny eggs in gold and silver paper while Lila and Grandma hurried around the kitchen with pots and dishes. Although Rosalind began to feel anxious about being away from home so long, she knew it would be rude to leave without joining in the meal. Besides, she was ravenous and needed to eat before the long walk back.

It seemed as if every few minutes the door was flung

open and more people crowded in to hug Selina and her family, wishing them a happy Easter. When Rosalind was introduced, some of them hugged her, too, while every single one said how pleased they were to have her with them on this special day. Rosalind had never felt so welcome anywhere and began to envy Selina for living in such a community where everyone seemed to belong and where kindness and love were shown to all.

One elderly man was given a special welcome amid teasing remarks. "You managed to make it in time then, Eli. Good thing you did. We need you to play for the sing-along. You must be ready for a decent meal."

The reason for this banter was lost on Rosalind, whose eyes nearly popped when she was invited to take her place at the table, where the enormous golden-brown turkey was displayed. Jake carved a generous serving for her, while Grandma sliced ham and handed her dishes of vegetables. She thought she would never get through the piles of food, but it was all so good and she was so hungry that she ate every morsel.

"Now what kind of pie do you like?" Lila asked, clearing Rosalind's plate away.

"I don't think I could—"

"Nonsense! You've got to try the pies. I'll cut a sliver from the apple and a bit of pecan to start with."

By the time Rosalind struggled through her dessert, more guests had arrived to take the places of those who had already eaten. This would be a good opportunity for slipping away, so she stood and whispered to Selina, "I really have to go. My mother might be worried about me. She doesn't know where I am."

"I'll walk part of the way with you."

They quickly put on their coats, and Rosalind thanked Grandma and Lila.

"Come anytime," the women replied warmly. "We'd be glad to have you."

When the door closed behind them, Grandma turned to her daughter-in-law. "Poor child. She could use a few more hot dinners."

"I'm glad Selina brought her," Lila said. "She seemed to enjoy herself. Just a second—Eli's finishing his third piece of pie. Maybe he'll drive them. I'm sure he came in that old car of his."

Selina and Rosalind had only gone a little way when a horn tooted and made them turn."

"It's Uncle Eli!" Selina cried. A smiling, wrinkled man leaned through the car window and asked, "Fancy a ride?"

Rosalind had never felt so grateful. She was tired, and her leg ached from so much walking earlier. The two girls piled into the back seat, and the car bumped and jolted along Africville's unpaved road. When they reached the smoother roads of Halifax's North End, Rosalind directed Eli to her house. She climbed out of the car, thanked him for the ride, and said goodbye to Selina.

"You should have stayed for the singalong. You missed hearing me play the piano," the old man teased.

Clutching her basket of chocolate eggs, Rosalind limped along the front path, praying her mother would still be asleep. After the warm friendliness of Africville, the prospect of the almost empty house depressed her. She turned her key in the lock and quietly pushed the door ajar. Her mother stood halfway down the stairs in a bathrobe. She was paler than usual, and her bottle-blond hair stuck out in a tangle around her face.

"Where on earth have you been?" she demanded angrily. "I've been worried sick!"

SIX

Selina was so tired on the Tuesday after the Easter break that no amount of calling woke her. It wasn't until her grandmother came upstairs banging a ladle on a skillet that she realized she had overslept. Leaping out of bed, she dressed and swallowed half a slice of toast before dashing out of the house, only to see the school bus pull away from the stop.

It must have come early, she thought, trying to excuse herself for missing it. *If I hurry, I might still make it on time.*

She swung her book bag onto her shoulders and began to run, thankful her load was light. She was approaching the road beside the prison grounds when a loud tooting and screeching of brakes again announced the arrival of Uncle Eli's ancient car. Thankfully Selina flung herself in beside the old man, who grinned and said, "Missed the bus, did you? Glad I happened to be passing."

The car drew up in front of school as the bell stopped ringing. Selina sprinted across the playground to join the end of the line before the last three students entered the door. She flung her coat on its hook and hurried along the corridor, looking anxiously for Rosalind, whom she expected to find waiting for her somewhere. When she reached the class, however, her friend was already seated in the front row. As soon as she saw Selina, who came forward smiling, she turned away to burrow in her book bag, ignoring Selina's cheery hello.

The announcement of "God Save the Queen" over the public-address system sent Selina scurrying to her own desk. As she began working through the math problems Miss Neill had written on the board when the students finished singing, she felt a stab of concern about her friend's attitude toward her.

Maybe she didn't hear me, she reasoned. *Maybe she was a bit annoyed because I was late. We'll sort things out at recess.*

The minute the bell rang, Rosalind rushed to be first to hand in her work, then slipped through the door without a backward glance. Selina hastily finished the last two questions and dashed after her. By the time she reached the outer door, though, Rosalind was over by the fence, as far from the building as possible. The girl looked lonely and pathetic, limping along in her blue coat, head bent into the wind.

"Aren't you coming to skip with us?" Andrea Morris asked as Selina darted past.

"I'll just be a minute," Selina said. Running after Rosalind, she called, "Wait up!"

Rosalind didn't look at her. She kept moving away

with uneven, determined steps. Selina didn't know what to do. She was missing precious skipping time, but she was worried by her friend's behaviour.

"Why are you over here?" a familiar voice behind her asked.

Selina turned to see Molly, whose usually smiling face wore a puzzled expression.

"I was following Rosalind. She visited us on Sunday and seemed to have a great time. All my folks made her real welcome, and now she won't even speak to me."

"I thought I saw her with you in church, but there was such a crowd I couldn't be sure. I couldn't find you afterward," Molly said, secretly relieved she would have Selina all to herself again.

"Did *you* have a good Easter?" Selina asked.

"Great! We had so much company! Six people stayed over Sunday night. My aunt and uncle from Truro only left yesterday afternoon."

When they reached the group of girls jumping in and out of the turning rope, Selina brushed aside her uneasiness about Rosalind. She and Molly were soon caught up in the excitement and skill of the game.

Later that morning, during a silent reading period, she went over to the class library to change her book. She was leafing through the well-worn volumes, hoping for something interesting she hadn't already read, when she became conscious of someone standing close to her. A single glance told her it was Rosalind, who seemed embarrassed and unwilling to face her. Selina turned, anxious to ask what was wrong, but the girl merely put her finger to her lips to indicate they had to be quiet, then dropped a note onto the open book in Selina's hand.

Selina snapped the book shut, trapping the bit of paper inside, and hurried back to her seat. She slid the note onto her lap, away from Miss Neill's watchful eye, and opened it. The message was written in Rosalind's neat, spidery handwriting:

I'm sorry, but I can't be your friend anymore. My mother was very angry with me for coming to your home without telling her, and she has forbidden me to have anything more to do with you.

Rosalind

P.S. Thank you for a lovely time on Sunday.

In fact, Avril Devereau had said a great deal when she learned where her daughter had been. Rosalind could usually cope with her mother's tantrums by hiding deep inside herself and trying hard not to listen. This time she had found it impossible to ignore the outburst, which had shocked and hurt her. She could still remember the hateful words.

You've been to Africville, the filthiest place on earth, where they have no running water and have to boil the water they do have? And you actually ate some of their food? It'll be a miracle if you don't get enteritis or worse! You're probably infested with lice at the very least. Go right upstairs and take a bath and wash your hair. Leave your clothes right where they are and I'll disinfect them this minute. And remember, I don't want you anywhere near that girl again.

As Rosalind had tried to comfort herself in the warm bath, tears had streamed down her face. It was useless to argue with her mother, who always insisted on having her own way, but how bitterly she resented losing the only real friend she had made since coming to Halifax. Whatever her mother had said about Africville, she didn't know what it was really like.

A wave of wistful sadness seeped through Rosalind every time she recalled the huge table with its spotless white cloth and dishes of beautifully cooked food that she had so enjoyed. It had been the best meal she ever remembered eating. And the community, where all the people cared for one another, had accepted her without question into its warmth and security, making her feel so happy for just a few short hours! If only Selina knew the heaviness in her heart as she obeyed her mother's orders and refused to speak to her former friend.

Selina was especially glad for the extra-long gym lesson that was announced that afternoon. Rosalind was never able to participate in gym classes and chose to remain in the classroom reading or doing her homework. As the students entered the gymnasium, they were surprised to find Mr. Fisk in quiet conversation with tall, dark-haired Mr. Ellis, the handsome young gym teacher.

When they were all sitting cross-legged on the floor, the principal said he had decided to accept a suggestion made to him by the gym teacher. "Mr. Ellis wants our grade six class to form an athletics team and accept an invitation to take part in a competition against the grade sixes from three other schools. This will mean a lot of hard work and extra practices, but we want everyone to be involved. The meet will be held in June at Buckingham School, where there's a large sports field." With these words Mr. Fisk disappeared, leaving Mr. Ellis to fill in the details.

50

"I'm not going to choose people for individual events yet," he said. "I want you all to get into good shape before we start time trials next month. I'm certain we can produce a really good team by the beginning of June."

Mr. Ellis then led them in a long exercise routine, starting with simple stretching skills and progressing first to slow arm and leg movements and finally to vigorous activities for the entire body. Selina joined in wholeheartedly, determined to qualify for as many races as possible. She was sure she was already fitter than many of the other kids who flopped down breathless when Mr. Ellis allowed a short rest. She decided that beginning today she would give up riding the school bus and would build up her stamina by running to and from school.

As soon as the bell rang that afternoon, she hurried off, anxious to try running the entire way home. She knew it would mean not starting too fast but keeping up an even rhythm. Selina was concentrating so hard that she didn't look up when the school bus passed her about halfway, and she missed Molly's frantic waving from the window.

Reaching the upper track quickly, Selina was leaping from tie to tie, congratulating herself on how well she was doing, when an unusual occurrence caused her first to slow down and then to stop completely. Two white men in smart suits were deep in conversation while they strolled across the rough bit of ground between two houses below her. At first she thought they were coming to tell her to get off the track, but they turned to the front door of one of the homes and knocked loudly. Selina knew that an elderly couple, Mr. and Mrs. Jenkins, lived there. She stared without any attempt to curb her curiosity as Mr. Jenkins answered the knock and began to talk to the men.

"Why'd you run off like that?" At the sound of the breathless voice she spun around to find Molly hurrying toward her. Molly had scooted back to meet Selina as soon as she was able to get off the school bus.

"I wanted to practise for the athletics team," Selina replied.

"What athletics team?"

"The one Mr. Ellis told us about today. We're going to compete with three other schools in June."

"We didn't have gym today," Molly said. "I hope my class has a chance to try out."

"I thought I'd train by running all the way home. I only stopped because something's going on. Look down there!"

Selina pointed to the two men, who were now circling Mr. Jenkins's property, peeking into the outhouse, glancing at the fenced piece of yard where he grew vegetables and flowers in summer, and shaking their heads at the notice by the water pump the Jenkinses shared with several other families. It read: PLEASE BOIL THIS WATER BEFORE DRINKING AND COOKING. Finally they returned to the elderly man waiting on his doorstep, where Mrs. Jenkins had joined him. Then all four disappeared inside the house.

"What do you make of that?" Selina asked as they set off again.

"Dunno, but guys like that scare me."

They walked in uneasy silence until they reached the spot where they had to part. Feeling guilty for bolting off earlier without a word to Molly, Selina suggested they play together later.

"Will you help me with my math homework?" Molly asked. "I don't think I can do it."

"Sure! Bring it over after supper."

Molly continued along the track, leaving Selina to dash down the hill in a final short spurt for her own back door, which she flung open as she wiped her feet on the outside mat.

"Guess what!" she said, confronting her grandmother and father, who were enjoying mugs of coffee at the kitchen table. They stopped their conversation and faced Selina expectantly. "Molly and me just saw two white men over at the Jenkins house. They looked like they might be from the city. They walked all over the property and checked the well, then went inside with Mr. and Mrs. Jenkins. What do you think they wanted?"

There was complete silence for a good half minute before Grandma banged down her coffee mug and uttered a long, low wail, quite the saddest sound Selina had ever heard. The old lady then pulled her apron over her face and laid her head on the table, sobbing as if her heart would break.

Selina stared beseechingly at her father, wondering what awful thing she had said to cause this reaction. He looked back at her reassuringly, mouthing the words "It's not your fault" before grasping his mother's hand across the table.

"Now, Ma," he said gently, "there's no need to get yourself in such a state. Nothing's happened yet."

"No, but it will! You know it will!" Grandma cried through even louder sobs.

Jake signalled to his daughter, who came forward hesitantly to put an arm around her grandmother's shoulders. The old lady flung down her apron to look up at Selina. "I been terrified this would happen. They're gettin' ready to move us out of here!"

"They can't do that, can they?" Selina asked, shocked.

"Rumours have been flying about for years," Jake said. "But they never amounted to anything. Recently they've become real persistent. There's all kinds of talk about why the city wants the land Africville stands on for its own use."

"This bit o' land is mine!" Grandma wailed.

"Sure it is," Jake soothed. "It was bought by my grandfather's father over a hundred years ago. When he died, it passed to Gramps, and he left it to you. The deed is right there in that drawer." He went over to the kitchen dresser and pulled a large, worn envelope from beneath a pile of tablecloths. "I don't see how anyone can argue with this evidence, even in court."

"How can Africville folk afford to go to court?" Hannah asked between sobs.

"I'd feel a lot more concerned if you didn't have this deed. Some of the folks around here don't have anything in writing, because they were granted land by those who first owned it. The city knows where to find them at tax time, though, and they always pay up."

"I don't trust anybody from the city one little bit. They're some smart, and they can twist things around and get their own way. Besides, there's talk goin' about that some folks is already negotiatin' for compensation from the city if they get themselves moved."

"Where did you hear that?" Jake asked.

"Over at Mamie Forrester's when I was there for the sewin' circle. She reckoned one or two families from round the turn is already interested in movin' if there's compensation to be had and the promise of somewhere decent to go."

"Don't listen to Mamie Forrester," Jake said, anxious to calm his mother's fears. "She's the biggest gossip I know. Besides, if I lived round the turn, I might even think about it myself. They get a lot more stink from the dump up that end of Africville."

"*You* wouldn't want to leave, would you?" Grandma asked.

"Course I wouldn't. This is our home, our community, but there are some things I'd sure like to see improved. That dump should never have been put so near people's homes. I'm just glad we still have our own good well water."

Heaving a deep sigh, Grandma got up from the table and went to the sink, where she started to peel potatoes for supper. When Jake seized two buckets and made for the door, Selina also grabbed a pail and followed him.

"You don't really think they'll make us move, Dad, do you?" she asked as they made their way to the well.

"A few months ago I would've said no, but a lot of people cave in when they're under pressure. We don't have money to pay lawyers to fight for us."

"Grandma's real upset."

"Sure she is. This house and the land it stands on mean everything to her.

"The kids at school say Africville was settled by folks who'd escaped slavery in America," Selina said.

"It's more complicated than that. My grandfather told me our people came to Nova Scotia at different times, like after the American Revolution and the War of 1812. Here they were free citizens and were granted land in various places. Over the years many of them moved to Africville to be near Halifax, where they had a better chance of finding work."

Selina didn't understand everything her father was saying, but was afraid she might cry if she asked him to explain further.

"Don't tell your grandma what I said about folks giving way under pressure," Jake said, turning the well handle. "We don't want her worrying any more than she needs to."

"I won't."

They filled their pails and paused for a moment to gaze at the houses that sprawled down the hillside to the darkening waters of the Basin. Sadness gripped Selina like a cold, heavy claw, so she hung back and let her father set off alone.

This was home. She knew everyone who lived here. This was her community where she was totally accepted for who she was. Despite the tumbledown, ragged look of some of the houses, despite the dump and the railway lines, Africville was a beautiful spot in which to live. Surely no one would be cruel enough to steal it from her people, especially from those whose families had lived here for over a hundred years. She picked up her pail and walked slowly back to the house, but try as she might, she couldn't smother her own smouldering fears.

SEVEN

Although the possibility of leaving Africville wasn't discussed again in Selina's presence, she sensed a nervous uncertainty beneath the surface of life at home. In contrast to this, the atmosphere at school was the happiest she had ever known. She enjoyed the challenge of increasingly difficult schoolwork, often gaining such high marks that Miss Neill singled her out for special praise. Selina was embarrassed by the teacher's comments at first, but learned to accept them. She sensed they helped her earn respect from the other students.

Along with the rest of the class, she looked forward to the gym lessons most of all, keeping up her own training by jogging to and from school instead of riding the bus. Extra practices were held outdoors on fine days, and Mr. Ellis soon noticed she was one of the most promising runners.

At first all the students trained for every race, but by the end of May, Mr. Ellis encouraged them to concentrate on their strongest events. Since it had been agreed that the whole class should participate, he was slow to make his final decisions, wanting to build up the best team possible. After lots of trials and a great deal of discussion with Miss Neill and Mr. Fisk, he finally posted the lists of names on the notice board near the cloakroom. Selina could hardly believe her eyes when she saw she was chosen for three events: the one-hundred and two-hundred-yard races, and the final leg of the relay.

"Will you be able to come and see me run?" she asked her parents and grandmother after telling them her news.

"Try to keep us away!" Jake said. "I'll trade a shift with one of the other porters."

"And I'll simply take a morning off," her mother declared, hugging her warmly. "Oh, honey, I'm so proud of you."

Only Grandma said nothing. She looked straight at Selina for a few seconds, then went over to the window and stared out. Selina was puzzled until she watched the old woman take hold of the corner of her apron and wipe it across her eyes.

"She's very happy for you," her father whispered.

Selina nodded uncertainly before going up to her room. Gazing over the rooftops, she wondered whether her grandmother was unwell. Suddenly an icy fear gripped her, tightening her stomach muscles and making her head swim. Had those men from the city been to *her* home? Was the threat of being forced to move creeping ever closer to her own front door? Angrily she dashed back downstairs, fled the house, and ran down the hill, across the lower rail line, and along the road below the church until she stood on the rocky bank above the water. Furiously she seized a heavy stone and flung it as far as she could into the sea, watching the ripples spread into bigger and bigger circles.

She picked up another stone and another, hurling them with all her might as she remembered uneasily the number of times adult conversation had ceased abruptly when she entered a room. There had been meetings at church, too. Her father had returned from one of those to slump bitterly into an armchair and hide behind a newspaper, while her grandmother sat at the kitchen table staring silently into space. Selina was mad at herself for being so involved in her own affairs, her school work, and all the extra sports practices. She had taken little notice of events that affected the people dearest to her.

Finally Selina became calmer and walked slowly back up the hill. When she opened the door, she heard voices raised in argument. She stood motionless, stunned by every word, horror and disbelief mounting inside her.

Her father's voice rising with frustration hit her first. "You know all those meetings got us nowhere. More folks are beginning to feel they'll be better off moving now that there's no chance of any improvements like water and sewers for Africville."

She was surprised to hear her mother add quietly, "If we do have to move, I guess I'll be a bit nearer to the tram for work."

"Is that all you can think about?" Grandma cried.

"No, Ma, I was just trying to see if any good might come out of leaving here."

"*Nothin'* good can ever come of it. This is where I

belong, and this is where I'm stayin'.'"

"Some folks are already making plans to leave," Jake said gently.

"And some will make a deal with anybody if they're given money to go," his mother snapped. "Nobody's gonna bribe me to move, no matter how much they offer, and they ain't offerin' much. It may look like a lot, but any fool can see it won't last five minutes if you're settin' up home in a new place where you have to pay rent."

Feeling she couldn't bear any more, Selina coughed and slipped inside, closing the door with a loud bang. The conversation ceased at once. Her mother began to lay the table for supper, which they ate in awkward silence. As soon as the meal was over, Selina went up to her room and lay on her bed, pretending to read.

When she flung back her bedroom curtains the following morning, which was Saturday, she pushed her doubts and fears of the previous evening to the back of her mind. Everything looked as it always did, the whole world so bright and beautiful in the early sunshine. The sky was the colour of the delphiniums that lined the side of the house in late summer, and the waters of Bedford Basin rippled gently with tiny whitecaps. How could anyone ever think of leaving here on a day like this?

After helping with the breakfast dishes and fetching a pail of water from the well, she settled down at the end of the kitchen table with her homework. While Selina wrestled with long division, her grandmother moved silently about the room. She stirred the crock of baked beans simmering since early morning and shaped loaves from the dough that had been rising in a huge bowl beside the stove. Baked beans and brown bread were a tradition for the Saturday meal. Today they would eat them for lunch, as Jake and Lila would both be home early.

At twelve o'clock, just as Selina finished memorizing a list of spellings, there was a light knock on the door. Before she had time to say "Come in!" Molly flung open the door and stood grinning on the doormat as she wiped her feet. These days she hardly saw Molly during the week, but they usually spent Saturday afternoons together, catching up on the news, sharing concerns and worries, always close even after a separation, the way good friends always are.

"Sit yourself down," Grandma said, opening the oven door to take out two golden-brown loaves, which she expertly tapped out of their pans and laid on a wire cooling rack.

She ladled bowls of beans and cut generous slices of bread. The two girls needed no encouragement and were soon ready for second helpings. Grandma sat down, too, with a bowl containing about a tablespoon of beans accompanied by half a slice from the loaf. She seemed to find it difficult to eat even this small amount, and stirred the contents of her bowl a great deal before raising the spoon to her lips.

The two friends exchanged puzzled glances but didn't comment. Selina, who knew this meal was usually a favourite with her grandmother, was once more seized with fear and uncertainty by the old lady's strange behaviour.

"Let's go out," Molly said, breaking the awkward silence.

Quickly they cleared their dishes, washing them in a bowl of warm water and leaving them to dry in the rack beside the sink. Grandma silently watched them leave without any of her usual warnings about keeping their eyes and ears open for approaching trains.

It was one of those late May days that made it seem as if summer had arrived early. As the two girls walked to Tibby's Pond, the sun shone so warmly that they removed their sweaters. By the time they reached the far side of the little bay, they were glad to sit on the shingle to cool off.

Molly began to pour out her fears about a forthcoming math test, so Selina offered to help her go over some of the examples in the book. They then sat quietly for a few minutes until Selina voiced her own concern for her grandmother.

"She hasn't been herself since the day I told her about those men visiting the Jenkins place. She got into a real state. She can't bear the thought of giving up her home."

"Has anyone from the city been to see your folks?"

"I don't know. I've been out a lot recently, and they don't say much in front of me, but Dad and Grandma were arguing last night. I've never heard them fight before. I think the whole idea is making her sick."

"Some guys came to my house. I'm not sure why. Us kids were sent out to play."

"Did your mother tell you anything about it afterward?"

"She wouldn't say a word, but that night I heard her and Dad talking for a long time after I went to bed," Molly said. "I know they worry about the water supply coming from that awful pump everybody else near us uses, too. It's such a nuisance having to boil it before we can drink it or cook with it."

"I guess we're lucky, having our own well. You don't really think your folks will agree to go?"

"I don't know, but I did hear Dad say the authorities

want to split Africville up. The idea makes me feel real terrible. I can't bear the thought of moving. I don't think I'd ever want to live anywhere else. It's so lovely and peaceful here." Molly sighed and leaned back on her elbows, gazing at the low hills surrounding the gently rippling stretch of Bedford Basin.

The nagging fear Selina had been trying to smother suddenly sprang forward again. She was certain now that her own family had been visited by local authorities. Why else would her grandmother, who had always been so strong, suddenly seem weak and vulnerable?

"Why don't we walk by the Jenkins place?" Molly suggested. "We saw the men from the city go into that house ourselves. If the Jenkinses are still there, we'll know things are okay for now at least."

They hurried to the group of houses where they had noticed the two men a few weeks earlier. As they approached, everything appeared just as it always had. Lines of washing flapped gently in the breeze beside houses that seemed to be enjoying a quiet nap in the early-afternoon sunshine.

"Nothing's changed here," Molly said.

"Maybe it's a big fuss about nothing. Africville's been here over a hundred years, my dad says. It's not going to be that easy to get rid of it," Selina added.

"I'm starving again. Let's go over and see Aunt Margaret. She's sure to be home, and she ought to have time for us today. I could eat a big slice of one of her banana cream pies."

Molly dashed away, getting a pretty good start on Selina, who followed and easily gained ground. She was just behind Molly when her friend pulled up so sharply that Selina crashed into the other girl's back.

"Why'd you stop like that?" Selina demanded angrily.

"Look at the house!" Molly said in such a strange tone that Selina felt quite scared.

Selina gasped. "It's all boarded up."

"Do you think she's died or something?"

"No, I bet she's moved. I overheard my folks say that some people were making deals with the city. They must think Africville can't survive, so they're taking whatever money they can get and letting themselves be put in other houses or apartments. It looks as if Aunt Margaret has done just that."

Slowly they made their way back to Selina's, neither of them able to think of anything to say. Of course, Aunt Margaret was only one person, and she was old and alone.

"I guess she could have gone to family or into an old folks' home," Selina whispered at last.

Molly nodded, but both knew this wasn't the case. If someone like Aunt Margaret left, others would surely follow. They walked on in silence until they reached the point where their paths diverged.

"See you at church tomorrow," Selina called as they parted. "I'll help you with your math afterward if you like."

She followed the uneven track slowly, resolving not to mention at home what she had just seen. There was no point in upsetting her grandmother any more than was necessary. She glanced over the fence of a nearby yard, where red tulips splashed a patch of colour beside a rough lawn that was already green. What would happen to all of this if they were forced to leave?

Below her stood the church, friendly and welcoming, the centre of everything. No one would ever dare harm the church. It was far too important, too sacred. If the church remained, then Africville would surely survive as a community, even if some people did leave. Reassured by this line of reasoning, Selina quickened her pace toward the warmth and security of the only home she had ever known, the only home she ever wanted.

EIGHT

Sunday was no longer an eagerly anticipated day of joyful celebration. Uncertainty about the future made everyone restless, not only at home but also at church, where even the hymn singing lacked its customary energy.

Although there was no formal meeting after the service, Selina noticed people were standing around in groups, speaking seriously and quietly to one another before going home. Only her grandmother pushed doggedly through the crowd, greeting old friends with the merest nod as she hurried away. Although they would have liked to stay and chat, Selina and her parents always followed closely behind Hannah, anxious not to cause her further distress.

Sunday supper, usually a highlight of the week, was eaten almost in silence by just the four of them, with no visitors creating the party atmosphere Selina loved. She looked forward to Monday morning as never before.

The track meet was to take place on Wednesday, so she knew there would be extra practices before then.

Another fine, sunny morning greeted her as she left the house and broke into a strong, rhythmic stride. She was in such good shape after the past weeks of training that she hardly gasped for breath, even when running uphill. She soon reached the higher railway track, where leaping from tie to tie was no effort at all.

Selina passed the place where she had seen the two men from the city a few weeks ago. The unexpected sight of a garbage truck skidding to a halt outside the Jenkins house, however, jolted her to a sudden stop. Hardly able to believe the scene unfolding before her, she watched Mr. and Mrs. Jenkins appear at their front door as two men climbed down from the vehicle. She heard voices raised in disagreement as Mr. Jenkins gestured angrily at the truck with his fist and Mrs. Jenkins put her apron to her eyes.

"I only know that we have orders to move you to Corby Street!" the driver shouted.

Selina didn't wait to listen further, but dashed blindly on, trying to regain the bounce in her step. She felt as if someone had thumped her in the stomach, while her face burned like fire. If the Jenkinses were leaving, how many more people from Africville would go? The thing that hurt her most was the thought of this quiet, kind elderly couple having their belongings loaded into an open garbage truck for the whole world to see. Garbage trucks only brought the things city people *didn't* want to the dump at the other end of Africville.

Despite stopping, she reached school in good time and stood beside a group of girls near the door.

"I guess there'll be extra gym today," Andrea Morris

remarked. "We need to practise our baton changes for the relay. I'm glad I'm in that. With you there we're sure to do well."

Selina nodded but didn't reply. She was still deeply troubled by what she had seen on her way to school, and couldn't help remembering Andrea's earlier unkindness. Out of the corner of her eye she noticed Rosalind standing by the fence at the edge of the playground, lonely and forlorn in a green dress with a frill at the hem. Selina's heart went out to her, but there was no way to speak to her now.

The ringing of the bell jerked Selina's attention away from sad thoughts, and she finally turned to Andrea to say, "Yes, we should practise the changes. We don't want to drop the baton."

She was soon swept up in the mounting excitement of the next two days. In addition to the extra practices with Mr. Ellis, everyone in the sprints spent recess trying to improve starting techniques. The students who were in the fun events, such as the three-legged and egg-and-spoon races, worked hard to avoid stumbling or dropping the precious eggs.

There was deep disappointment when light rain began to fall on Tuesday afternoon, but tremendous relief when Wednesday dawned bright and clear with hardly any wind. As soon as attendance was taken, the students clambered into the bus that took the Mayfield team over to Buckingham School.

They arrived to find the other two visiting teams already there and all the Buckingham students lining the track, which had been freshly marked on the field beside the school. Almost before they had time to take off their sweaters, a call for those in the hundred-yard dash could be heard over the loudspeaker.

Selina took several deep breaths as she nervously walked to the starting line. She caught sight of her parents, who were standing about halfway along the track.

The pistol cracked and Selina streaked away, looking straight ahead, ignoring the other runners, though she could feel those on either side close on her heels. All too soon they were nearing the tape and she saw to her dismay that the girl on her right, running for Buckingham, was just in front of her. With a final, supreme effort Selina put on a last spurt of speed to break the tape fractionally ahead of her rival. There was a cheer from all her teammates as the result was confirmed on the loudspeaker.

Afterward Selina joined the other girls from Mayfield to watch the hurdle races and some of the novelty races that followed. They all kept a close watch on the scoreboard, and it soon became obvious that none of the schools would be an easy overall winner. Each of the four teams posted victories in two events, though Mayfield crept slightly ahead on points by never being lower than second in any race.

Remembering how close her first finish had been, Selina felt even more anxious when the time came to take her place for the two-hundred-yard race. At the sound of the starting gun she shot ahead and kept a fast, even pace throughout. But she was unable to put on the extra burst needed to claim victory, which narrowly went to her close rival from before. Now Mayfield and Buckingham were equal in points and stayed neck and neck until all events except the girls' relay were completed.

Excitement was at a peak as the four runners on

each team took their places in specially marked sections around the track. Each competitor was to run a distance of one hundred yards, and Selina was determined to give every ounce of energy she could muster when her turn came to run the fourth and final leg. With mounting tension she watched as her team battled to stay ahead of the home team, who were being cheered loudly by their whole school. The first two baton changes went without a hitch, and she stood ready to break into a run and gain as much speed as she could before grasping the baton from Andrea. It was here that the long hours of practice paid off, for the other team slowed during the final exchange, allowing Selina to streak ahead to victory. Since the relay carried extra points, Mayfield became the overall winner.

For a few minutes Selina joined her mother and father, who were standing a little apart from everyone else.

"We're so proud of you," Lila said, hugging her warmly.

"Where's Grandma?"

"She felt it was a bit too far for her to manage on such a warm day," her father answered hastily.

"She said to wish you the very best," her mother added.

Their conversation was cut short by a voice over the loudspeaker introducing a member of the school board, who gave a brief speech congratulating all the participants on a sportingly contested event. When he held up the cup for the winning team, Mr. Fisk signalled to Selina that she should step forward to receive it. Smiling broadly, Selina raised the trophy high above her head, and turned to face her parents. She then joined her class to climb happily into the bus for the ride back to school.

"My mom said if we won I could have a party tomorrow

afternoon for all the girls on the team," Andrea announced as they ate their bag lunches in the classroom.

There was a loud cheer followed by excited chattering. Only Selina remained silent. She had never been to a party at one of the white kids' homes and couldn't be certain she was really included. She wasn't sure if she wanted to go, but Andrea looked across at her and said, "It's too far for you to go home to change after school. You'd better come ready so you can come straight to my house."

"Of course you should go, honey," her mother said when Selina voiced her doubts at home. "If you don't have a good time, you can always leave. They may think it impolite if you don't show up. I'll wash and iron your white dress right now. Come home for lunch so you can change, and we'll ask Uncle Eli to drive you back."

Again Selina said nothing, but her anxiety mounted throughout the rest of the evening and the whole of the following morning. In addition to a natural shyness about visiting Andrea's house, she felt certain her lovely white dress would be quite wrong for the party. But what else could she wear? Apart from the blouses and skirts Grandma always kept neat and clean for school, and her old play clothes, the white dress was her only really good outfit.

The following afternoon she put it on, covering as much of it as possible with a long jacket-sweater belonging to her mother. There were a few stares but no remarks when she entered the playground and took her place in line. Although the classroom was hot, she kept the sweater on, anxious not to draw attention to herself.

As soon as the bell rang for the end of classes, the

girls quickly put away their books and hurried off. Several of them lived near the school and dropped by their homes to change, so Selina found herself reluctantly accompanying Andrea along a road that skirted one side of the school. After about five minutes, they crossed the pavement and headed for a quiet side road lined with shady laburnum trees covered with dangling yellow blossoms. Halfway along this road, Andrea turned into the small front yard of a three-story house with a glass porch. The moment they mounted the steps, the front door flew open and Mrs. Morris came out to meet them.

She was a small, brown-haired woman with an oval face and pale complexion. Two spots of rouge, inexpertly applied to her cheeks, made Selina think of a doll she had once owned. The girls followed her indoors, where she suggested Selina wait in the living room while Andrea changed. She then made a hasty exit.

Although Mrs. Morris was perfectly polite, Selina sensed a certain embarrassment in her manner. *Andrea's mother doesn't really want me here,* she thought as she sat in an armchair near the partition that separated the living room from the dining room. This was folded back today, so she could see the big table laid with a lace cloth, crystal glasses, and white plates rimmed with gold.

The furniture in both rooms looked old and heavy to Selina, very different from the modern things in Rosalind's home. She wondered if it were valuable, for it shone from many waxings and hardly seemed to have been used despite its age. She caught sight of another woman carrying a plate of sandwiches to the table. The woman gave Selina an inquisitive glance before rushing away.

Selina stood, stepped into the dining room, and crept toward a door in the far corner of the room. She pretended to be looking at a painting of some apples in a bowl, but really she was drawn by the sound of voices. One was clearly Andrea's mother's, the other presumably that of the woman she had just seen. From the clatter of dishes she could tell the two were working in the kitchen.

"She looks quite clean and she's very nicely dressed," the woman said, "I guess you couldn't really leave her out."

"No, she did very well in the races yesterday, and Andrea was asking all the other girls. Albert's not pleased about her being here, though. He thinks the people in Africville are better to stay all together."

"I agree with him. They're surely happier with their own kind, just as we are. It's a pity they lost their own school. It must be ten years since it was closed. I think it would be better if they could still be educated in their own community instead of having to come up to Mayfield by bus."

"Andrea says this girl's very smart, so maybe she's getting a better education in our school," Mrs. Morris said.

"How's she going to get home this evening?"

"Walk, I guess."

"And cross those railway lines? I'd never have a minute's peace if a child of mine were doing that! Of course, there's talk that Africville won't be there much longer."

"Are you sure about that?" Mrs. Morris asked. "I would think they'd fight to keep their homes. After all, they've been there a long time."

"I know someone whose husband works at city hall.

She reckons some of the people have moved out already while they can get a deal from the city. With all the rumours of another bridge over to Dartmouth, not to mention development along the shore, that land may be needed."

At that moment the doorbell rang and Andrea came dashing downstairs to answer it. When she heard more voices, Selina slipped through the living room to join the others, who were taking off their coats in the hall. She stood at the edge of the crowd, relieved to see several of them in party dresses but horrified to find they were leaving umbrellas to dry on the porch. Her concern about getting home without ruining her dress made her push the awful things she had heard to the back of her mind.

"You'll have to play in the basement while we finish preparing the food," Andrea's mother said, emerging from the kitchen.

"Who's the lady helping your mother?" Selina asked as they all clattered downstairs.

Andrea pulled down the corners of her mouth before replying, "That's Aunt Freda, my dad's sister. She always shows up if there's anything going on here, poking her nose in. She won't help much, and she'll make sure she leaves before dish-washing time."

For half an hour the girls took turns at table tennis, a game Selina had never tried before. She soon began to enjoy it and quickly became quite adept at hitting the ball. Those waiting their turn danced to a Beatles record until a man's voice called them to come and eat.

Throughout the meal Selina sat quietly, always remembering to say please and thank you but never joining in the conversation, which gradually got louder as the girls became more excited. She couldn't help noticing that Mr. Morris never once looked in her direction, though he joked with some of the girls he obviously knew well.

After the meal, when they all stuffed down as much cake and ice cream as they could manage, he suggested they sit on the floor in the living room while he went to find his magic wand. For half an hour he entertained them with conjuring tricks, inviting one girl or another to choose a card or hold a ball or place an egg in a bag for him. Here again he ignored Selina, though she clapped as hard as the rest when a trick was successfully completed.

She became increasingly miserable at this treatment, especially when she recalled overhearing that Mr. Morris hadn't wanted her there at all. Selina found herself blinking back tears when she thought of the remarks Aunt Freda had made about Africville. Mrs. Morris was at least polite, if a little chilly in her manner. Selina stood and went nervously over to her.

"I really think I should be going. I have a long walk," she said, looking the woman straight in the eye.

Mrs. Morris could hardly conceal her relief as she accompanied Selina to the door to a chorus of goodbyes from the others, who were now settling down to watch television. The rain was drumming against the windows when they stepped onto the porch among the drying umbrellas.

"Oh, dear!" Mrs. Morris said. "You don't have a coat. You'll get soaked."

Selina snuggled into her sweater and buttoned it up to her chin. She had her hand on the porch door before the woman added reluctantly, "There's an old umbrella in the corner there. Why don't you borrow that. Make sure you bring it back and give it to Andrea tomorrow."

"I will," Selina said. "Thanks for a lovely time. The food was delicious. You must have gone to a lot of trouble."

Mrs. Morris eyed her suspiciously, but there was no trace of sauciness in Selina's voice. Uneasily she watched the girl skirt past the car parked in the driveway, knowing her husband would never allow her to drive Selina home. "I bet he'll take all the other kids, though," she muttered, following the progress of the umbrella until it disappeared around the corner.

While Mrs. Morris washed the dishes—alone as Andrea had predicted—she admitted to herself that the black girl had been beautifully dressed and extremely well mannered.

"She thanked me most politely when she left," she remarked to her husband, who joined her a few moments later to dry some plates. "Do you think they'll move them out of Africville? Freda does. She thinks the city may want the land for a new bridge."

"She could be right. I don't think they can stay there much longer, anyway. It's a real slum."

"Where do you think they'll put them?"

"I don't know, and I don't care, as long as they don't resettle any of them near us. The value of our house would go right down."

By now Selina had reached the first of the railway tracks. She hopped nimbly to one side to avoid a passenger train rumbling by. Despite the sharp wind tossing the rain into her face and making it difficult for her to hold the umbrella, her spirits rose the nearer she got to her house.

The knowledge that she would always be loved here

soothed the pain she had suffered but didn't take it away completely. It worried her a great deal to hear that Africville's days were numbered from someone who didn't even live there. She tried to imagine a second bridge spanning the harbour from Halifax to Dartmouth but couldn't. Who needed another bridge, anyway? In frustration she closed the unruly umbrella before thrusting her head forward against the driving rain for the rest of the walk home.

NINE

Now that the sports meet was over, Selina decided to give herself a break from training. After what happened at the party, she longed for the comfort of spending as much time as possible with Molly. The next morning she left home early and headed for the bus stop, looking anxiously for her friend, who came running excitedly toward her the minute she saw her.

"It's great to have you back on the bus with me!" Molly said as they clambered aboard and claimed seats together.

When they arrived at the playground, Selina hung back from joining a game of tag with Andrea and her group, even though several of the girls called to her.

"Don't you want to play with them?" Molly asked, puzzled.

"I'd rather stay with you."

"How was the party?"

"Okay, I guess, but I didn't like Andrea's parents. Her

father was real mean to me."

Their conversation was interrupted by the bell, which sent each of them dashing to her own line. During the rest of the morning, Selina had little time to think about anything except work, for exams were only ten days away. There were still new topics to be covered before Miss Neill could begin reviewing material from earlier in the year.

I'll never remember it all, Selina thought, wrinkling her forehead as she pored over some fractions the teacher had just explained.

Molly was waiting for her at recess, her normally cheerful face tense with worry. "I simply can't understand long multiplication, and it's going to be on the exams," she moaned. "You'll help me, won't you?"

"I'll try, but I have to do my own homework first. You'd never believe how much stuff Miss Neill is trying to get through. Make sure you know your multiplication tables, and you'll find things a lot easier."

With so much crammed into lessons, and evenings taken up by revision, the days flew by. Selina even studied for much of the weekend, though she made time to help Molly on Saturday afternoon. All too soon she was sitting in class on Monday morning, ready to begin the first exam, which was English, her favourite subject. Other subjects followed over the course of the week, and by three-thirty on Friday afternoon everyone heaved a sigh of relief when the last paper was collected.

As she passed Rosalind's desk on her way out of the classroom, Selina was surprised by a weak smile from her former friend, who whispered, "The exams weren't too bad, were they?"

"N-no!" Selina stammered, too stunned to stop and

make further conversation.

All that remained was the picking up of report cards the following Tuesday. There was a brief assembly that morning, during which Mr. Fisk wished everyone a happy holiday. Excitement was mixed with apprehension as the students returned to their classrooms to collect the report cards in sealed envelopes. Selina could hardly wait to get home so she could find out what her grades were.

"I know the envelope will be addressed to your mother and me, but you and Grandma can open it together," her father had said. "It's not fair to make you wait till we come home from work."

Selina watched impatiently as her grandmother fumbled with the flap of the envelope with her gnarled, rheumatic fingers. Finally, unable to wait any longer, Selina snatched it from her and slit across the flap with a small paring knife. Together they examined the white card to find that it contained no grade lower than A–. Most were straight A's, and there was one A+, a grade rarely awarded, for essay writing.

Selina danced gleefully around the room, but her grandmother sank heavily into a chair by the table, staring at the card in her hand and shaking her head as if she couldn't believe her eyes.

"What does the writin' at the bottom say?" she asked at last. "I can't see too good."

"It says, 'Selina is a well-mannered, conscientious student who has made excellent progress,'" Selina told her, knowing her grandmother could read very little.

A broad smile now replaced Hannah's dour expression as she slowly realized how well Selina had done. "You surely did us proud. You make certain now that you go right on and finish high school. You'll be the first one of this family ever to do that. Who knows? You might even make it to college. Wouldn't that be somethin'!"

Supper that evening was such a happy event that everyone seemed to forget about Africville's troubles. Jake and Lila returned from work to find Grandma putting the frosting on her special carrot cake, which was to follow Selina's favourite crispy chicken.

"Get yourself a good education and you'll never look back," her mother said when they were almost finished. "You don't want to have to take the sort of job I do day after day."

***

At first it seemed summer vacation would be as perfect as it was every year. Selina and Molly were inseparable, inventing all kinds of games as they played outdoors in the bright summer weather. On wet days they learned to knit or make cookies under Grandma's watchful eye. Sometimes they joined in baseball games with Molly's brother and his friends or swam and begged rides on the raft the boys floated in Tibby's Pond at high tide. The beach here was still their favourite place for exchanging secrets or just idling away hot afternoons.

One particularly fine morning they prepared a picnic lunch, saying they were going to hike to the section of Africville farthest from home.

"I can't imagine why you want to walk over there," Grandma declared as the girls stuffed things into their backpacks. "Just make sure you stay away from the dump. The stink is terrible there, 'specially this time o' year, and you could easily pick up some disease."

The girls glanced meaningfully at each other but didn't reply, knowing the hike would provide a perfect excuse for a detour to the dump. It was generally accepted that items from the dump could be repaired and put to good use by Africville residents, who kept a keen eye on garbage trucks as they made their way through the community. Recently a load of toys had been spotted, and Molly was anxious to see if any of these could be salvaged.

"My brother says they were only dumped last night," she whispered. "I hope we can find something nice to play with."

The two set off, following a small path through a patch of woodland that grew between their own part of the community, always referred to as "up the road," and the area known as "round the turn." Just beyond the edge of the trees they pulled up short, their pleasure in the day's adventure destroyed. A green house with boarded-up windows stood in their way.

"Oh, no!" Molly sighed. "Someone else has moved."

Selina stared in disbelief as they approached the house. "They can't have been gone long. There are carrots and beans growing in the garden. They must have decided to leave in a hurry."

The two girls passed several other homes that seemed inhabited still, though there was no sign of life. The whole area drowsed in the hot noon sunshine with only the distant cry of a seagull breaking the silence.

"Look over there!" Molly said. "I know there were more houses last time I was here."

Slowly they approached the area Molly indicated and found themselves face-to-face with piles of rubble where several homes had stood.

"These houses have been knocked down!" Selina said, shocked. "The ones left look strange and lonely without them. I don't like the feel of this place."

Molly shuddered. "Me, neither. It makes me feel all creepy. There's no way people can come back to Africville once their houses are destroyed."

"Let's go home," Selina said. "I don't care about toys." She felt ready to weep.

Molly turned, wrinkling her nose. "I can smell the dump. With the wind blowing up from the Basin the stink's real strong."

They hurried back along the path through the trees, not speaking a word. Selina's throat was so tight, she could hardly breathe. Silently she prayed that no one else would move, especially from her section of Africville. The two girls had no heart for games the rest of that day but lounged listlessly around the house, getting in Hannah's way and making her wonder if they were sick.

The following morning Molly appeared on Selina's doorstep soon after eight o'clock.

"What got you up so early?" Selina asked, shuffling sleepily downstairs in her pajamas.

Molly didn't reply but jerked her head backward as a signal for her friend to come outside. As soon as Selina closed the door behind her, Molly's face crinkled with sadness and two huge tears rolled down her cheeks. She tried to speak several times, but the words only came out as sobs. Selina, who had never seen her sunny-tempered friend in such distress, finally understood.

"You're leaving, aren't you?" she asked. "Oh, no! You can't!"

Molly could only nod in reply and cover her face, and Selina found herself choking back tears, too.

"When are you going?" she asked as they clung to each other.

"A week Monday," Molly whispered.

"That's only ten days away!"

"I know," Molly sobbed. "We won't even be able to play together for the rest of the summer."

"Where are you going?"

"Truro, to our relatives there. We'll stay with them till we can find a place of our own."

"That's too far away!" Selina wailed, tears streaming down her own face now.

"Maybe you could visit us," Molly suggested wistfully.

"Even if I do it won't be the same! You'll find new friends and forget about me."

"You know that's not true!" Molly declared, overwhelmed at the depth of her friend's sadness and anger. "I can't stay now. There's so much to do at home. I promise I'll come over this afternoon if I can."

Selina turned indoors. The hateful menace that was destroying Africville was coming ever closer. For the first time she acknowledged that she and her family might have to face moving.

"What's wrong?" her mother asked, spreading margarine onto a slice of toast at the kitchen table.

"Molly came over to tell me they're leaving."

Lila poured herself a cup of coffee from the pot on the stove. "I thought they might. So many folks are coming around to it."

"What about us? Grandma won't leave, and this is her house."

"We may have to persuade her in the end. If everyone else goes, we won't be able to stay."

"Where *is* Grandma?" Selina asked, realizing for the

first time she could remember that the old woman wasn't in the kitchen preparing breakfast for everyone.

"I told her to stay in bed. She's complained of one or two headaches recently, and yesterday she said she had a pain in her chest. She refuses to go to a doctor, so I feel the best thing for her is to rest."

"And she agreed? That's not like Grandma."

"No, it certainly isn't. Maybe you could take her a cup of tea in a little while and see if she wants anything else. I have to run, or I'll miss my tram."

After watching her mother hurry away, Selina helped herself to toast and marmalade and cleared the breakfast dishes before going upstairs to get dressed. She lay on her bed with a book for about an hour, trying to read, but found it difficult to concentrate. The same thoughts echoed through her head: *Would she be moving like Molly? Was her mother really serious about going? Where would they go? What would it be like?*

At last she crept downstairs and put on the kettle to make a pot of tea. She placed one of the best china cups on a lace doily on a small round tray and poured the tea, hot and strong the way Grandma liked it. Carrying the tray upstairs, she knocked timidly on the bedroom door. Hannah was propped against her pillows, looking much smaller in the high bed than she did when she bustled about the kitchen.

"That looks nice," she greeted Selina.

"What would you like to eat? I could fix us some lunch soon."

"Nothin', thank you. I'll rest a bit longer."

Anxiously Selina retreated to make herself a peanut-butter-and-jelly sandwich. She poured a glass of milk and sat at the kitchen table but had difficulty swallowing even small bites of food. The house was far too quiet, and now, added to her concern about moving, was a new worry about her grandmother. Selina desperately hoped there was nothing seriously wrong with her.

She pushed her plate away and paced around the room, staring at familiar objects—photographs on the wall, the vase of lilac blossoms on a table by the window, even the pots on the stove—in an effort to reassure herself nothing was changing. It was no use. Everything seemed unreal, like a horrible, unending nightmare.

TEN

The long afternoon stretched depressingly ahead, and Selina wondered how she would get through it alone. To her enormous relief Molly staggered into the kitchen about a half hour later without even knocking. She looked hot and tired as she slumped into a chair. "I've been helping Mom pack all morning. She's given me the afternoon off while they take some stuff over to Truro."

"What shall we do?"

"Give me a few minutes, then we'll go over to Tibby's Pond. I'm too tired to walk far."

Selina washed and dried two apples, and they set off slowly for their favourite spot above the pond. Here, too, it was unusually quiet, for the tide was out and no one was swimming or playing with a raft. Neither of them spoke while they munched on their apples and watched the gulls wheeling in the wind. While Molly dozed, Selina stared at the familiar outline of low hills fringing the distant shores of Bedford Basin and gradually felt calmer, almost reassured. Everything looked just the same as it always had, and no one could alter this wonderful view.

They were suddenly startled by someone calling Selina's name. She stood and was astonished to see Rosalind hurrying eagerly toward them, swaying unsteadily from side to side. A man was standing beside a car parked at the edge of the dirt road above the pond. As Rosalind approached, Selina could see she looked happier than ever before. She was smiling broadly, and the pinched, anxious expression had vanished from her face. Rosalind was wearing neat red cotton slacks and a simple white top, so different from the fussy dresses Selina remembered.

"I'm leaving this weekend for Toronto," she explained the minute she reached them. "I just had to say good-bye." She pointed toward the man. "My father's come for me. He's arranged to have treatment for my arm and leg. I'll live with him and go to a clinic every day for therapy."

Selina was so astonished at seeing her former friend that she didn't know how to reply. Rosalind seemed to understand and continued. "I was so sorry about what happened. It was all my mother's doing. When Dad asked me if there was anyone I wanted to see before I left, I told him you were the only real friend I made here. He said at once that he'd bring me to see you. We were driving to your house, but I spotted you from the car. I had such a wonderful time the day of the Sunrise Service. I wish I could come again sometime."

"There may not be another," Selina said.

"But surely—"

"A lot of people are moving out of Africville," Molly

explained. "My family's going next week."

"How come?"

"The city authorities say it will be better for us."

Rosalind turned to Selina and asked, "What about you?"

"We're not fixed on leaving. I think my parents might agree, but my grandmother won't budge. She gets in a state at the idea of losing her home."

"That's too bad. I really liked her. She was so kind to me."

"Is your mother going to Toronto with you?" Selina asked.

Rosalind's smile faded for a moment. "Not right away, but Dad thinks she'll join us soon. I have to go now. I'll always remember you. Goodbye, and good luck!"

She turned to climb laboriously back to the waiting car. Her father hurried to meet her, grasping her hand to help her along. They both waved before climbing into the waiting vehicle, which turned and jolted back the way it had come.

"We'd better go, too," Selina said. "Grandma's not well. I need to be home to start supper."

"I'll come with you and give you a hand," Molly offered. "My folks won't be back for ages yet."

They set off slowly, each of them wondering what it would be like when they could no longer be there together. Tibby's Pond meant so much to them.

To their surprise Hannah was sitting at the kitchen table when they entered, cutting squares for a quilt she was sewing. "I heard you both go out," she said, smiling warmly. "I figured I ought to be up and about when you got back."

"You're feeling better?" Selina asked, relieved to see her grandmother active and cheerful once more.

"Sure am! I had a good long rest, and now I'm ready for work again."

"Is there anything we can do to help you?" Molly asked.

"Well, about half an hour ago I saw Anita James goin' by with a pail full o' blueberries. They're ripe already and real good this year. If you two could pick me some, I could bake a few pies."

"It's too hot for baking," Selina said.

"Don't worry! I won't put the oven on till I start supper. You girls needn't hurry. Help yourselves to a Popsicle and go sit in the shade at the side of the house."

Several Popsicles later, when the sun began to slip down the sky and the breeze from the ocean felt pleasantly cool, the two friends climbed the slope behind Africville, where blueberries grew in thick patches. The first few bushes they came to had already been picked clean, so they pushed their way into a clump higher up the hill. Twigs and thorns plucked at their clothes and scratched their legs, but they took little notice. The berries were some of the best Selina ever remembered —big and juicy with wonderful mauve skin. She popped several into her mouth, and they oozed the sweetest juice imaginable, staining her lips and tongue.

Better not eat too many until the pail is full, she told herself firmly as she placed her pail beside her and settled down on her heels to concentrate on stripping the short, laden twigs.

Selina gathered every ripe berry within easy reach before standing to stretch farther over the low bushes until she was right on the tips of her toes. A sudden shriek from Molly, who was busy a few feet away, made her lose her balance and topple headlong into the middle of the patch, scratching her arms as she fell.

"Did you have to yell like that?" Selina called, turning anxiously to make sure her precious pail of berries was still upright.

"I've scratched my hand and it hurts," Molly said. "It's bleeding!"

Selina struggled to her feet. "Let me see."

Molly held out her plump little hand. A few small red beads oozed slowly from the back of it, below the knuckle of her middle finger. "What am I going to do?"

"It's not much. Just suck on it."

"I can't. It'll make me throw up." Molly watched the small spots of blood run together.

Selina turned to go back to her picking, only to notice a red smear on her own pink shirt. When she held up her left arm, she noted that one of her own scratches had also drawn blood just above her elbow, a place impossible to reach with her mouth.

"I'm going to wait till the bleeding stops before I pick any more," Molly said, making for the edge of the clump of bushes.

Selina followed, and the two of them cautiously eased themselves onto the grass, holding their wounds away from their clothes.

"We won't be able to do this together again," Selina said suddenly. "I'll hate blueberrying without you."

"Me, too. I don't even know if there'll be any berries where I'm going. You won't ever forget me, will you?"

"Never! You're more like a sister than a friend."

"Even though we're not blood relatives?"

"Sure! Wait a minute. We can make ourselves blood sisters. Take a bit of the blood from my scratch, and I'll take a spot of yours."

Molly hesitated before gently wiping her little finger along the scratch on her friend's arm. Selina dabbed her own pinkie in the spot of blood on Molly's hand.

Each girl then rubbed the blood of the other into her own so that the two were well and truly mixed.

"Ugh," Molly groaned, pulling a face. "That's disgusting!"

Selina tried to smile but felt hot tears welling at the edges of her eyelids.

Molly put an arm around her. "We really are sisters now," she whispered sadly.

"And we always will be, no matter how far away from each other we have to live," Selina agreed, returning the hug.

They sat quietly for several minutes, eyes on the blue water shining below the roofs of Africville. From up here everything looked as it always had, but they knew nothing was the same. Molly wondered what life would be like in Truro. She'd enjoyed her few visits to her relatives there, but the idea of starting at a new school without any of the people she knew terrified her.

Selina's thoughts were on Africville. How much longer could she and her family go on living here now that so many people were moving? Would Grandma ever be persuaded to leave, or would they find themselves living in a ghost town? The thought of a community in which all the houses were flattened except her own frightened Selina. She stood up in an attempt to push away this terrifying image.

"Come on," she said. "We'll never fill our pails at this rate."

They worked hard for the next half hour, hardly saying a word and ignoring the growing stiffness in their backs and knees.

"I can't fit another berry in this pail. They keep rolling off the top," Molly declared at last.

"Why don't you eat a few? I'm going to." Selina stuffed a handful into her mouth.

Slowly they began the walk home, taking care not to spill any of the precious fruit but stopping occasionally to nibble a few more berries. When they reached the point on the road nearest to Molly's home, she handed her pail to Selina.

"Can you carry these as well as your own?" she asked.

"I guess so, but won't you be staying for supper with us?"

"No, I'd better get back. I ought to start fixing something for Mom and Dad. They'll be home around eight."

Selina crept along extra cautiously, a pail in each hand, until she reached her house. Putting one pail on the doorstep so she could open the screen door with her free hand, she took the first lot of berries indoors. She placed them on the kitchen table and went back for the second pail.

It was only when she put it safely beside the first pail that she realized how quiet the house was. She had expected to find her grandmother in the kitchen with pastry prepared, anxious to wash the berries and put them into a pie, but there was no sign of her, nor of any preparations for baking or supper.

Maybe she decided to take a nap, after all, Selina thought. *I bet she slept longer than she intended.*

She went to the foot of the stairs and listened, but there was no sound. "Grandma, I'm home. It's getting late," she called.

There was neither shuffle nor murmur above, so Selina started to climb the stairs, stopping every few steps to call out again. There was still no answer, and she began to feel uneasy. Grandma was a light sleeper and usually woke at the slightest noise.

Maybe she was feeling better and went out for a walk, Selina told herself, though this possibility didn't convince her. Grandma never went out unless she had a reason. Surely she wouldn't go outdoors on such a hot day.

Selina hesitated at the top of the stairs before knocking gently on her grandmother's door. When there was no reply, she timidly turned the handle and opened the door a crack. Hannah Palmer was slumped facedown on the floor beside her bed, one hand clutching the edge of the patchwork quilt she had been trying to fold back before climbing up to rest. She didn't move a muscle in response to Selina's terrified shrieks of "Grandma! Grandma!" Nor did she hear her granddaughter's ear-piercing scream as Selina sprinted down the stairs and fled the house in search of help.

ELEVEN

Although she tried many times to remember clearly what happened during the hour or two after she found her grandmother, Selina could never be certain her dreadful memories were accurate. She knew she had run out of the house and grabbed the arm of the first person she saw, screaming uncontrollably at him that her grandmother had fallen and he must call her father and mother. It wasn't until two days later that she learned the astonished stranger had been on his way to play baseball with his Africville friends when she demanded his help.

Realizing something was seriously wrong, the young man had followed her indoors and up the stairs. As soon as he saw the motionless figure, he went in search of neighbours, one of whom must have telephoned Lila at work. Selina remembered hurling herself at her mother, who arrived by taxi. Before going indoors Lila held her daughter tight for several minutes.

After that the house was full of people, many of them weeping openly as they tried to offer help. Several ladies followed her mother upstairs, and there were whispered remarks about "laying her out," which Selina didn't understand. Trying to find a spot where she could be alone, she went outside and flung herself on the grass in the shadows. From time to time she heard the murmur of voices and the sounds made by cars coming and going, but she took no notice. Hours later, when the long summer evening finally cooled and it was quite dark, her father found her. Uncle Eli had driven to the railway terminal to meet him on his return from working a run to Toronto.

Jake crouched beside her and said gently, "You know how determined Grandma was never to leave this house. She even made me promise she would be buried straight from home. The men from the funeral home have laid her out on her bed for tonight. Tomorrow she'll be put in her coffin and stay in her room until she's taken to the church for the funeral."

He put his arms around Selina and pulled her to her feet, whispering, "Molly's mom's here. She's come to see if you'd like to stay with them tonight, seeing as Grandma's..." Fighting back tears, he couldn't trust himself to say any more.

Selina nodded dumbly. Dad understood she would find it impossible to sleep in her own room next to her grandmother's. Even at Molly's she slept badly, tossing and turning long after her friend had drifted off. Despite being busy with preparations for their move, Molly's family treated her with every kindness, insisting she sleep at their home until after the funeral.

The next two days passed in a flurry of preparations.

The round of visitors continued, many of them bringing food and staying to help her mother clean the house or do the laundry. Nothing felt right. Instead of the normal secure and comfortable feeling of home, everything was different. The house looked the same, except for the huge bouquets of flowers in every room, but Grandma's place in the kitchen was taken by a succession of strangers, unceremoniously handling her pots and pans. Selina found it difficult not to tell some of the women to take extra care with her grandmother's best dishes.

On the evening before the service she decided she would steel herself to go upstairs to view her grandmother's body, something she had been avoiding.

"Would you like me to come up with you?" her father asked.

"No thanks. I'd like to go alone."

"There's no need to feel afraid."

Selina tiptoed quietly up the steep stairs and turned the handle, pushing the door of Grandma's room gently ajar and standing still for a moment while she plucked up courage to go in. Although summer-evening silence had settled over her own part of Africville, the distant shouts of children playing at the beach reached her through the open window. She held her breath as she approached the coffin, a simple but good one of dark maple, as her grandmother had requested.

Selina wasn't sure what she had expected, but when she looked at the still, smooth features of her grandmother, she had quite a shock. This wasn't the wrinkled face of the elderly woman who had laboured day after day for others. It was the face of someone much younger, with no trace of the worries that had troubled her over the past months.

Selina stared in disbelief. "You look so peaceful,"she whispered. "Wherever you are, you must be very happy. Now you won't ever have to leave Africville."

The rumble of a passing freight train shook the little house. "I bet you don't hear that noise anymore," Selina said. "I'll never stop missing you, but I'm certain you're better off where you are."

Flinging herself to her knees beside the bed, she offered up a heartfelt prayer of thanks for her grandmother's life. "God help me to be strong, whatever happens," she breathed as she got to her feet, feeling strangely calm.

The day of the funeral was the hardest she had ever lived through. Family and friends began arriving soon after breakfast, some crowding indoors, others standing around outside. When Selina went up to her room to get ready, she gazed through the window and was surprised to see three black limousines beside the house as well as the hearse. Several other cars were parked along the road below the lower track, while people were walking quietly toward the church.

She took her white dress down from the closet, and the awful tide of grief she had somehow held back flooded her. Throwing herself facedown on her bed, she sobbed as though her heart would break. "Oh, Grandma, Grandma! Why did you have to leave us? What am I going to do without you?"

A thousand images of her grandmother crowded her mind. Hannah had always been there when she fell and grazed a knee, always had lunch ready on the table, always knew instinctively when something was wrong.

"It's time to get ready, honey," said Lila, who had quietly entered and was choking back her own tears at the sight of her daughter's distress.

Selina allowed her mother to pull her gently to her feet and slip the white dress over her head. Mutely she turned while Lila tied the bow at the back. The memory of her grandmother she had been trying so hard to avoid confronted her, of the day when they went to town to buy the lace and ribbon for the dress, the very same day Grandma had shown up at school in time to rescue her from the vicious attack. She sobbed more bitterly than before. "Grandma knew when I needed her," she said, clinging to her mother. "She always knew."

"She wouldn't want you to grieve like this," her mother said, guiding her to the top of the stairs. "Try to remember the good times. Hold fast to those."

Clinging tightly to her mother's hand, Selina followed her father outside. Her grandmother's coffin, now covered with flowers, was already in the hearse at the head of the line, and she wondered vaguely who had carried it there. Silently her father held open the door of the first car so she and her mother could take their places. How strange it seemed to drive the short journey to the church when she always walked to services!

The organ was playing softly as they entered to follow the coffin and take their places at the front, Selina weeping softly, Lila with her head bent to avoid pitying glances, and Jake upright, his face as still as carved ebony.

Selina felt she was gliding through the service in a waking dream of hymns and prayers. She was thankful when the time came for the sermon so she could sit and close her eyes. As the minister described her grandmother's tremendous contribution to her family, friends, church, and Africville, she listened intently, oddly comforted by his words.

"Hannah Palmer lived through some of the best times of our community and through its declining years," the minister concluded. "But never did she cease to love and serve it with all her heart. May God grant her eternal rest and peace. We will now sing 'Amazing Grace,' which was one of her favourites."

From the conviction with which the hymn was sung, it seemed to Selina that the whole congregation was trying to show deep love and respect for her grandmother. She tried to join in at the beginning of each verse but couldn't produce a single sound, though she knew all the words by heart. Tears blurred her eyes, and her throat was so tight she thought she would choke.

After the minister's blessing, it was time to follow the coffin outside. Selina again took her place in the waiting limousine for the slow drive to Fairview Cemetery at the head of the long procession of cars. The crowd stood quietly around the open grave while the coffin was lowered and the final prayers were said.

No sooner had they returned home than the first of a seemingly unending line of mourners arrived to express their sympathy. Selina stood beside her parents, receiving hugs and kisses from one after another, some of whom were total strangers. Feeling faint from the heat in the crowded little house, she eventually excused herself to go to her room, where she lay down fully clothed and wept silently.

A light tap followed by the door opening made her jump. Molly crept toward the bed, looking unusually serious. "I have to leave now," she said. "We're driving up to Truro with a load of stuff. I'm not coming back. They're leaving me there to stay with my aunt and uncle. The moving van is coming tomorrow for the rest of our things."

Selina sat up and clung desperately to her friend. "Were you in church? I didn't see you."

"We only just made it. We had to stand at the back, but we came over to the cemetery, too."

"You can't go like this! What am I going to do without you?"

"We'll keep in touch. I'll send my address. I can write a lot better now. You'll write back, won't you?"

Selina nodded, not trusting herself to speak.

"Molly! Molly!"

At the sound of her father calling impatiently from the bottom of the stairs Molly released herself from her friend's arms and backed toward the door.

"I've got to go," she whispered. "But whatever happens I'll always be your blood sister." With that she turned and fled, leaving Selina on her bed crying bitterly again.

Sometime later, when she was lying half asleep, the door opened once more and her mother tiptoed to the bed, carrying a plate and a glass of milk. "You haven't eaten a thing, honey. I brought you some cherry pie and one or two squares."

Selina sat up and sipped the milk before nibbling on a Nanaimo bar.

"Most of the folks have gone," her mother said. "There are just one or two of the women helping me clean up. Come down if you feel like it. It's been a hard day."

Selina nodded. "I wish Molly didn't have to go. I wish she could stay a bit longer."

"I know, but you'd still have to part. Think of it this way—maybe if you have all the sorrow together, things will be brighter all at once, too."

Selina finished the food her mother had brought but

didn't go downstairs. Instead she undressed and crawled into bed. Worn out by sudden loss and overwhelming sorrow, she fell into a deep, dreamless slumber.

TWELVE

When Selina went downstairs the following morning, she was surprised to find both her parents calmly eating pancakes and drinking coffee. As soon as she appeared, her mother poured batter into the skillet to fry some for her.

"You're not going to work?" Selina asked, taking her place at the table.

"No, I'm taking some time off while we get things sorted out," Lila replied.

"And I'm taking some of the vacation I'm entitled to," her father added. "This morning we're all going to see an apartment."

"You mean we're moving?"

Jake sighed. "It's the only way. Africville's not going to survive. Several folks who were here for the funeral are moving, too. We might as well go now rather than wait till we're forced out."

As soon as the breakfast dishes were cleared, they

set out for the tram terminal. Selina, who was surprised they weren't walking the whole way, enjoyed the unusual experience of riding with both her parents.

The apartment was really the top half of a house something like Andrea Morris's, though not nearly so well kept. There had originally been four bedrooms, but one was now a kitchen and one a living room, leaving two bedrooms. There was also, to Selina's delight, a small bathroom made from a walk-in closet, complete with a claw-foot tub. When she tried the taps at the sink, hot and cold water gushed freely.

"I'll be able to take a bath every day," she said excitedly.

"Maybe," Lila cautioned, "but hot water doesn't come cheap, and we'll be paying rent to live here. We never had to do that before."

"Do you think Mrs. James might give you a raise?"

"That old skinflint! I don't think I'll go back to house-keeping for her. I may advertise for daily cleaning and take in a bit of sewing."

Selina stared at her in surprise. "I didn't know you could sew."

"I always used to make my own clothes, and things for my mother and sister, but when I married your dad, Grandma did the sewing, same as she looked after the house. I'll enjoy getting back to doing some myself, and some of the cooking."

There was no sign of resentment in Lila's voice, but Selina couldn't help wondering whether her mother had been totally happy with their previous arrangements. It would be great if she wasn't away so much, especially now.

"Don't get me wrong," Lila continued. "I was very fond of your grandmother, and working all those years gave me the chance to put a little money by, even after we paid all our bills. Now I can take time to decide when I'll go back to work."

Everything moved rapidly after that. They spent several days sorting and packing their possessions, agonizing over what to take and what to give or throw away. They also made a number of journeys to the new place, struggling under the weight of bags and boxes. Selina and her mother cleaned the rooms from top to bottom, scrubbing and polishing until everything shone.

Early one morning the shrill toot of a horn announced the arrival of the city truck that was to take their furniture to the new apartment. Selina shuddered at the thought of all their worldly goods being loaded in broad daylight for everyone to see and was relieved when her mother suggested the two of them should go on ahead while her father helped the driver.

They worked so hard that everything was in order in a few days and the apartment began to feel less strange. Selina enjoyed unpacking some of their well-loved possessions and finding new homes for them.

About a week after the move her mother roused her soon after eight o'clock one morning. "A lady just called about the ad I put in the paper. She's been sick and needs someone to help her out right away. She sounded very nice. You'll be okay while I'm away, won't you?"

"Where's Dad?"

"He was called in to work. They were short-staffed, so they asked him to go back a day early."

"I'll be fine," Selina mumbled drowsily.

At first she thought she would go back to sleep, but when she couldn't, she climbed out of bed and went to her window. It was at the back of the house overlooking a small, narrow yard. A clump of foxgloves struggled through the weeds of an overgrown flowerbed beside a dried-up lawn. At the end of the lawn a wooden fence separated this yard from the yard of the house opposite, whose back bedroom faced her own. As far as she could see in either direction, there were similar small yards, all crowded side by side between the backs of the rows of houses.

A sudden sensation of claustrophobia seized Selina, and she backed away from the window. Where was that lovely free feeling she always associated with home? Where was the sea? Where was the rumble of the railway that made the house shudder? She wandered into the living room, but the view from there of the fronts of the houses was equally depressing. The homes in long, straight rows were all similar to one another, not scattered higgledy-piggledy on the hillside like those in Africville, where no two were alike.

Selina pulled on some clothes and washed her face. Without stopping for breakfast she went downstairs and let herself out the front door, making sure it was locked behind her.

She hurried along past a dozen streets all like her own until she reached Barrington, where she turned left toward familiar territory. The sight of Bedford Basin glinting in the sunlight made her smile, and when she arrived at the place where the pavement ended and the dirt road began, she broke into a run. Soon she reached the first set of tracks and began striding along the ties, her spirits soaring at the feel of the breeze on her face as it tossed her hair behind her. A familiar distant rumble sent her leaping aside to wave vigorously at the driver of the passing train before hurrying on again. Her feet now seemed to fly faster and faster the closer she came to *home.*

Reaching the point where she always turned downhill toward her grandmother's house, she stopped in total astonishment, wondering if she had missed her way. She gazed around in horror, but there was absolutely no doubt. The house wasn't there, nor were several others that had stood nearby. Rubble and broken pieces of wood littered the entire area.

Selina staggered to the place where she had lived for so long. She sank to the ground, feeling faint and giddy. All around her lay familiar fragments of her old home. Part of the kitchen sink stood on its end beside a heap of broken glass. A torn piece of rose-patterned wallpaper from her grandmother's bedroom lay pinned by a section of door frame.

Totally overwhelmed, she struggled unsteadily to her feet, unwilling to stay a moment longer. Tears blurred her eyes as she reeled helplessly away. She would go to the church. If it was locked, she could sit on the steps outside and compose herself before returning to the apartment. She stumbled to the bottom of the hill in a daze and turned to where the familiar refuge would welcome her with its protection. As she blinked the tears away, however, all she could see was a huge empty space. *Even the church was gone!* No longer would its bell summon her to attend worship, surrounded by loving friends and neighbours.

Sick to her stomach, Selina spun on her heel and bolted, almost colliding with an old man walking slowly with the aid of a cane.

"Look where you're going," he said, stepping to one side.

"The church is gone," Selina gasped.

The old man nodded, bowing his head and leaning on his cane with both hands. When he finally spoke, it was in a small, strangled voice, so desperately sad that Selina could feel his grief welling up from deep inside. "They came and flattened it last night. How could anyone have so little respect for our place of worship? Soon there'll be nothing left of Africville. I'll have to leave, and I don't know where to go."

"We moved at the end of last week."

The old man raised his head, letting the tears run unchecked down his face. "You're Hannah Palmer's grandchild, aren't you?"

Selina nodded, looking directly at him for the first time and realizing she had often seen him in church, always on his own.

"Your grandmother was a fine woman, one of the best. Her heart would have been broken if she'd seen her home and church destroyed."

Selina didn't trust herself to reply. She turned to climb the hill once more, silently admitting that Grandma was better off than the old man. *At least she was able to have her funeral in the church*, she thought. *It must have been one of the last services held there.*

Leaving Africville's dirt roads for the pavements of North End Halifax, she now knew there was nothing to draw her back to her old home. She had to do her best to settle in the apartment, even though she felt imprisoned there. Before she could put her key in the lock, the front door flew open.

"I wondered where you were," Lila said anxiously.

"I went ho— I mean, I went to Africville. The house is gone and even the church. There's hardly anything left."

Her mother didn't reply but led the way to the kitchen, where they sat at the table to eat soup and muffins.

"I think I'll like working for the lady I went to today," Lila remarked after a few moments of uneasy silence. "She wants me twice a week and is recommending me to some friends."

"That's great!"

"She paid me well, so I thought we might go downtown this afternoon. We could get your school supplies and maybe some new shoes."

For a moment Selina said nothing, remembering she had always undertaken these expeditions with her grandmother. As if reading her thoughts, Lila continued, "I think you and I should do more things together. If we finish our shopping in good time, we'll treat ourselves to a ride to Point Pleasant Park."

"I don't think I've ever been there."

"It's near where I used to work, right by the sea."

Selina stood up and smiled eagerly. "I'll get ready."

"Better wash your feet and put on some clean socks, honey."

While Selina ran hot water in the bathroom sink, she decided that not everything in this new life would be bad. She would always miss Africville and her grandmother. They would hold a special place deep in her heart, a place to be revisited in her mind whenever she felt the need.

Now there were new things to look forward to, new challenges to be met at school, and a new and precious relationship with her mother. She hurried to her bedroom and put on a clean dress and socks. Grabbing a light sweater, she skipped to the top of the stairs to find

Lila already waiting in the hallway below. Selina took hold of the bannister and began to run lightly down the steps.

"I'm ready," she said, smiling. "Let's go!"